THE SPY IN 3B

COVERT AFFAIRS
BOOK 1

NANA MALONE

COPYRIGHT

The Spy in 3B

Cover Art by Nail Qambar

Photographer: Brandon Sosa

Cover Model: Nana Malone

Edited by Angie Ramey

Published in the United States of America

1

LYRA

I tried not to fidget in my seat as Roslyn James droned on and on about the mission.

The target location. Target resistance. Acquire the target. And oh yes, *don't kill the target*. That last part was especially important, considering the last mission where I'd run into a spot of trouble and nearly killed the target... accidentally on purpose.

"Am I boring you, Lyra?"

I wrangled my wayward attention and shook my head as I glanced around at my teammates. "No, sorry, Roslyn. I'm not bored at all."

Lies. I was bored stiff.

This meeting was part mission brief, part lecture. And I'd had one too many lectures lately.

"Look, we hear you. Don't kill the target. But to be fair, the last target was holding one of the girls hostage. He was a human trafficker, and I *did* save her life."

Roz sighed then gave me that subtle Michelle Obama-style lip purse that conveyed her displeasure but also her slight amusement. I really shouldn't take advantage of her being my mentor, but Sampson had that knife wound coming.

She dismissed the rest of my team, and when I pushed on the arms of the orange Tom Dixon designer chair to join them, she lifted her brow at me. "No, you stay."

Addie Franklin, my best friend and sometimes partner, gave me a wincing smile and then mouthed, *Good luck.*

Help that she was.

I turned back to Roz. "I'm so sorry. Look, I know you would like me to be more contrite about the Sampson mission, but I can't seem to muster any remorse. He was a human trafficker."

She expelled another long-suffering sigh and then placed her hands palms down onto the sculpted glass top of her Nina Campbell desk that was both functional and beautiful. "I don't know how many times I have to tell you this, Lyra. You need to tuck away your emotions. You're one of the best agents we have. But still, I have to lecture you because sometimes your emotions get the best of you."

I did push out of my chair then. If she was planning on continuing the lecture, I wasn't just going to sit down and take it. Besides, I was restless. I had a date planned, one I wasn't sure I wanted to go on. I started to pace around Roz's office, and she eased back into her chair. "Lyra, what's wrong? I spoke to Everly. She said you were edgy, tight. Is there something you want to share with me?"

Everly Jones was our in-house psychiatrist. We each saw her quarterly for evaluations, and if one of us had an 'incident,' we saw her more frequently. At that point, I was seeing her weekly.

I bit on the corner of my Pink Perfection polished thumbnail and frowned down at the acrylics. God, I hated acrylic nails, but they were part of the facade. Part of the costume. *This* costume, anyway. The carefree, have-no-worries woman. "I'm sorry. You're right. I shouldn't have disposed of Sampson so efficiently."

Roz's lips twitched then, and I could see the burgeoning grin forming. "Yes, Lyra. Wound him. Maim him. But we needed him alive."

"Roz, what he was doing to that girl, what he would have done to so many others... I just— He had her by the throat, and the next thing I knew, my knife flew out of my hand."

She shook her head at me. "Excuse me? 'Next thing you knew'? I know for a fact, Lyra, when you are in the mood, you have the utmost control. It's just that you never seem to be in the mood lately. You have gone quite righteous on us. You do know what we do here, right?" She spread her arms. "At The Firm, you know your purpose."

I grinned at that. "We keep the world safe." I sniffed and muttered the part I hated. The part that kept me up at night. "Sometimes we deal with shitty people to get what we need." I inhaled sharply. "I *could* show restraint. But when it comes to scum, restraint isn't really my strongest asset."

She sighed. "I know you could. You're just choosing not to. And it makes me wonder why. I thought you were happy doing this job."

I blinked rapidly. "What? Of course, I am happy." The Firm was my home.

We were a hidden government black ops organization that was so covert even the world's best hackers couldn't find us.

Our official cover was P.O.P. PR & Marketing. With its bright white, orange, and pink decor, our front offices looked the part of every other contemporary marketing firm. We "specialized" in businesses run by women. And the funny thing was, we actually did have marketing people on staff. On the off-chance that someone actually did try to hire us for a PR job, there were three people on the team that could put together a real pitch and get the job done.

I'd been recruited by The Firm when I was nineteen, a year after my parents died. I'd been lost and on the verge of my life imploding. That's how Roz found me. I'd worked here officially since my twenty-first birthday. And before that, The Firm had paid for my last two years of school.

I'd been alone and drifting, not knowing where my life was going to take me. She had given me purpose. I owed her for that, and I needed to be more grateful.

You also erased everything you were.

"I'm sorry. I really am. And you're right; I'm a professional, damn it. I just... Sampson was going to kill her, and I knew I *could* stop it, so I did. Because sometimes, we have to make a human choice."

She nodded. "Your humanity and your love of people is one of the reasons I recruited you. We don't want those qualities eliminated. I just want you to be aware that *the mission comes first.* You have to know that. You have to drill it into your bones."

"I hear you. I'm sorry." It was a real effort not to sound like I was choking on the apology.

Because I wasn't *that* sorry about what happened with Sampson and the not-so-accidental stabbing. It was more that I was sorry that Roz was disappointed in me.

"Okay, that's it." She stood, and I went to give her a hug. Sometimes, when I was feeling all alone, it was easy to pretend that Roz was my mother, though I knew she wasn't.

My mother had been very, very different from Roz. All warmth and softness, but sadly, a little afraid of her own child. She'd had her hands full with a daughter like me. I was always running off to save someone or to give someone a piece of my mind. By the time I was ten, I'd had several adults threaten to spank me if she wouldn't do it. Especially when she took me back to Ghana where she'd grown up.

Since I was a child, my mouth had always gotten the better of me.

My abhorrence of injustice started early. When something wasn't right, I *had* to fix it, even if fixing it meant I was likely going to get in trouble. What I wouldn't have given to hear my mother yell out one more time, *Lyra, for the love of Christ, be careful. Watch your mouth.*

But she'd been gone a long time now. I cleared my throat to dislodge the unexpected emotion. "I'm sorry, Roz. Next time, I will be full-on Elsa. Completely chilled out."

Roz shook her head at me, and then we hugged. I teetered on my heels, nearly knocking us both over. I managed to find my center of balance, but not before toppling several files on Roz's desk. One folder, much thicker than the others, flew open, and papers went everywhere.

Roz's voice was a swarm of harsh pinpricks as I bent to retrieve them. "Fuck, Lyra, leave it. Those are classified."

I bent down immediately. "I'm not even looking at them. I'm just helping you pick them up. I'm sorry."

She shooed me aside and shook her head at me. "No, I will get them. I said they're classified."

"Sorry." I backed off and put my hands up. "I was only trying to help."

She sighed. "Lyra, what's wrong with you? You seem off."

"No, I'm fine."

She lifted her brow and frowned at me.

I threw up my hands and then slid off the heels I was wearing. "These. These are the problem. I have a stupid date tonight."

She grinned at me. "Ah, yes. The nice boy from next door."

I laughed. "Roz, he's not a nice boy. He's a *man*. A full-fledged man." With the big hands of a man. Not that I'd been watching him too closely.

She nodded. "Yes, of course. Sorry."

I laughed. "Oh, you know what I mean. He's a man, and this is our third date, and I don't know what I'm going to do with him."

She laughed. "Well, it's been a while since I've been on a date, but I seem to recall that what you do with them is fuck their brains out."

My jaw fell open. "Roz."

"What? I was young once."

Screw *young*. Rumor was, in the past, she liked to try out the young Valentine operatives. A test drive so to speak.

I kept my amused snort to myself. "I have no objections to him, really. He's perfectly nice, I guess."

Marcus looked the part. Sex appeal *and* brains in spades. He was a game designer, and I liked him. He was kind, attentive, and conscientious. But there was something *off*.

Sometimes when we were together, it was like I ran into static interference. I could tell there was so much more to him, but if I went a layer too deep, it was like I had the wrong signal or something. And it certainly didn't help that our first two dates had been interrupted and we hadn't even kissed.

Roz smiled and nodded. "Yes, nice is good. You do need a

life outside of The Firm, so this is perfect. And you know that senior management prefers our agents in relationships."

Ahh, yes. The partnership clause. I personally found it bizarre. One would think black-ops agents should be unattached. But no, senior management found that agents in a steady, committed relationship performed better and were less volatile, so they encouraged partners. Granted, they did *not* encourage telling your partner what you actually did for a living. If you did... Well, that had grave consequences.

"I mean, do you think it's wise, all things considered?"

She picked up her papers and stacked them back on her desk. "In your case, yes. You had a different induction into The Firm. Before you joined us, your home life was a much more normal situation than some of our other agents. So get a life. Go on a date. Make some friends. Los Angeles is full of people looking to connect. Some of your teammates didn't have normal recruitments, whatever normal means. They had more *colorful* inductions into The Firm, but I even encourage socializing for them. So, you should date. And a relationship is a good way to release some of your... *tension*. It'll give you something else to focus on, so you'll be less of a crusader on missions. You'll take less unnecessary risks."

I sighed. I knew exactly what she meant by *tension*. "I know." I just didn't know what she meant by normal. How normal could I feel when everything about me was a lie?

My first name was real. My mother had seen it in a book and loved it. But my real surname had been scrubbed six years ago. Lyra Adamson was long dead. And Lyra Wilkinson was just an imaginary woman.

The cognitive dissonance lately had started to mess with my equilibrium.

It was encouraged for us to have lives, partners, etcetera.

Obviously, secrecy was of the utmost importance, but none-theless, we were urged to have relationships outside of work. It just got complicated. I'd seen it. Because love demanded honesty. *Love.* I wasn't in danger of that happening to me.

"Honey, when was the last time you had sex?"

I blinked rapidly. "Roz, you are *not* my mother."

"But I might as well be. When was the last time?"

A flush crept up my neck. "I don't remember."

She sighed. "I wonder if I should have handled the Tyler situation better."

I shifted uncomfortably on my feet. "We don't need to talk about that." Tyler was my ex and a subject better left undis-cussed. "I'd rather not talk about my sex life with you."

She pshawed me. "Think of me like the cool older sister."

"Fine, Roz, you're my cool older sister. Now, can we stop talking about this?"

"Okay, fine. Go have fun on your date. And Lyra, I think it's in your best interest to enjoy yourself with this young man. That dating app matched you, right?"

"Yes, it did." Lost in Love was the app, and I regretted ever signing up for the stupid thing.

"Then trust the process."

"Oh my God, you've been watching *The Bachelor*, haven't you?"

She winked at me. "Even I have a life."

Roz had been married to her husband, Adam, for four-teen years. He knew nothing about her actual job, and I never understood how they managed it. But she seemed to care about him in some sense. So if she could do it, I could do it. Besides, Marcus was nice. He was great. Just, um...

Boring.

"Okay, thanks for the advice. I love you, and I'll see you later."

"Yes, see you later. Have fun. Use a condom."

I whirled around and threw my hands up. "Roz."

She laughed at me. "Sorry, sorry. I'm just saying, safety is sexy."

I put my hands on my ears and hummed out *la-la-la-la* as I laughed. A quick check of my watch told me if I left now I'd get there right on time. We were meeting at a bistro not too far from our apartment building. Our first date was a shocker when I realized that I'd seen him before and he was actually my neighbor. I grabbed my purse from my desk and sighed at the picture of my mother and father. It was one of the few memories I kept of them. They'd had that kind of sweeping love that every little girl dreams about. And I just wished that one day I could have something like that.

Who knows? Maybe today is your day.

Marcus

"Where are we now, mate?"

My brother and I had been over this dozens of times, but somehow, he always seemed to forget.

"You know I can't tell you that."

"Right. Top secret."

"Yep, mate, top secret." It didn't matter how many times we'd been over this. It didn't matter that Liam was ex-SIS himself. He still asked. All he knew was that I was a government contractor. That was all he was allowed to know.

I changed the subject like I'd grown used to doing. If he pressed, I'd have to put on the façade. And there were some people I just wanted to be real with. "How's it going with you?"

"Ella is a beauty. When are you coming home to see her?"

I was up for leave in a few weeks, but I wasn't exactly enthusiastic about going home. Watching everyone do the *having kids and moving on with their lives* thing as their next step wasn't really something I was looking forward to.

Sooner or later, you must return home.

I knew it was true. I did have to go home at some point, but not today. Too many painful memories. "She looks beautiful in the pictures, mate."

"Thanks. Thankfully, she looks like her mum."

I laughed. "Yes, I would agree. Ella is going to be a beautiful princess."

"She needs her uncle to spoil her rotten and to help me build a tower to keep out suitors."

"Oh, I fully intend to spoil her rotten. That's what being an uncle is all about. As soon as I get leave, I'll come home. I need to cuddle that face." The lie tasted bitter on my tongue.

His brow furrowed "You all right?" he asked.

That was the problem with talking to Liam. Other than Dad, he was the only one who could see when I was full of shit. And that was why I had to get off the phone. The video chat was good though. It was good to see him with baby Ella strapped to his chest with some kind of contraption.

Slowly, he rolled them both back and forth as I attempted to change the subject again. "How come you only call me when you've managed to lull her into sleep?"

"Once she's asleep, a bomb could go off and she won't wake... unless of course you stop rocking her. I'm just more efficient at it than Taryn is. The wheelchair makes it easy."

I rolled my eyes. "Leave it to you to find a way to get extra cuddles in."

"Hey, Taryn was hogging her with all the breastfeeding. I needed to find a way to get in the extra time. Popping wheelies is something my very capable, gorgeous, and exhausted wife can't do."

"Well, good on you. I'll check in with you later. I need to get ready for my date anyway."

His grin split his face wide. "At bloody last. You can finally get a leg over. How long has it been since someone other than yourself touched your dick?"

I feigned shock. "Your bloody daughter is right there, mate."

"One, she's asleep. Two, I will teach her to never touch a dick. Three, don't change the subject."

I made a static sound. "Oh no. *Sssssss.* Going through a tunnel. *Ssssss.* Can't hear you. I'll call you later." More static.

He glowered at me. "You're in your damn flat. I—"

I hung up on Liam with a chuckle. That odd, hollow feeling settled in my chest again. It wasn't so much that I wanted Liam's life. I liked my life. I'd had a good life. Supposedly retired from active duty after 'incredible service.' Her Majesty the Queen had actually said that to me. But when I took the clandestine assignment with Exodus, I had no idea what I was in for. Six years. Six years of never even really understanding how I ended up here... alone.

Not that it wasn't encouraged to have a family, to have a life. It actually was. It looked better for a cover. But I couldn't get over the imminent danger I'd be imposing. But still, Exodus fully encouraged all employees to 'look the part.' Which meant having a girlfriend. A wife. And it wasn't the lying that held me back. I could lie all day. I looked at it as putting on a new skin. It was more that I wanted just one person I could be real with. One person I didn't have to pretend with. Was it so wrong that I actually wanted to care about someone? To actually want a connection with them?

Not to mention, my life was too dangerous, period. What if I couldn't keep them safe?

Connection gets people killed.

Which was probably why I'd been dragging my feet about this date with my neighbor. I'd joined a dating app, just to make it look like I was complying. I didn't want Exodus in my love life any more than I wanted my mother in it, but a few dates here and there kept up appearances.

Except the dating app I'd picked seemed to fall a little short. It had paired me with a woman who lived across the way in my building. And don't get me wrong; she was a stunner. A full mouth, light brown skin, a mass of curls that looked like they desperately needed tugging, and the kind of smile that could stop your heart. Not to mention her body. Jesus Christ, her fucking body. Curves that had to be cupped. Long athletic legs. She also had this quiet strength about her.

But despite her meeting every criteria I'd given the app, on our dates, she was... I didn't know how to describe it... all surface. I didn't need some kind of heavy emotional connection to want into her knickers, but fuck, *some* connection would have been nice. And to make matters worse, I could tell she wasn't exactly enthused by me either. It wasn't like I could actually *be myself.*

Our first two dates had been interrupted. The first when she'd had some work emergency. A pop star needed some crisis managed, so she'd run off from our bowling date with her phone to her ear. Just as well, since she'd been kicking my arse.

During our second date, Exodus had gotten a lead on the terrorist, Mikhail Bronstein. It was all hands on deck, so I'd been called in just after our movie at Griffith Observatory and hadn't even gotten to kiss her properly. The best excuse I could make under the circumstances was to feign food poisoning and put her in a cab without me. She'd almost refused and wanted to accompany me to the hospital. I was surprised she'd even agreed to a third date after that, but she came by the next day with soup and saltines and a sports drink to help with the dehydration for the food poisoning I didn't really have. I found I wanted to see her again.

She was just a straightforward, good person. The kind of person I should be with under other circumstances. To her, I was Marcus Black, a video game designer. It was a great cover and the kind of job that allowed me to travel but mostly work from home. And it was low profile. It gave me all sorts of reasons to not be available. It would be difficult to lie to her though.

There was a knock on my door, and I frowned. My other neighbor, Mrs. Washington, liked to check on me a lot. She'd always been a little nosy, which frankly, I didn't mind because I knew she was just lonely. But she had a tendency to chat for long periods, and as I had a date that night with Lyra, I didn't really have time. But still, I went to the door because she was a nice old lady who tried hard.

But when I checked the security monitor, I frowned then reluctantly dragged the door open to find my best mate and partner, Rhodes Matheson. "What are you doing here?"

"I'm here to give you a pep talk for your date."

I frowned. "You know I don't *need* a pep talk, right?"

Rhodes shoved by me regardless. "Yes, you do. You know Exodus doesn't like it when our agents don't comply."

I frowned. "They're saying I'm being uncompliant?"

He laughed. "Nah, I was just messing with you."

I flipped him off as I jogged into my bedroom to grab my jumper.

I didn't want to go too formal. It was our third date. I didn't want to signal that I expected anything from her.

I was under the distinct impression she had made up her mind about me. Hell, we hadn't even kissed.

I yelled at Rhodes from the bedroom. "Don't be a twat. I know it's hard for you but just try."

He chuckled at that. "Nah. I was actually here to pick up the SRP case file."

Sangita Rollins Polytech. One of their prominent physicists had vanished. My team was meant to find her and bring her back. I'd been doing a data analysis. And since it was an off-book mission. the senior board at Exodus wanted it untraceable, so we had paper files.

I nodded even though he couldn't see me. "Analysis is on my desk. I've memorized the profile."

I could almost hear his eye roll as I checked my appearance in my mirror. "Damn you and your photographic memory," he said. "Do you have everything you need?"

"I could use more ammo."

"I brought you a pack from Andreas."

"Excellent." Andreas Tomms was our weapons guy. Normally a courier delivered our packs to us, everything we needed. We only went to headquarters for briefings, training, and evaluations. Once our missions were assigned, we were left on our own. Like independent contractors.

"So, is tonight the night?"

The way he said it in that sing-song voice made me want to smack him. "Not the way you think, I'm sure."

"What, you don't like her? The Marcus I knew had such a way with the ladies." He grinned briefly, then his expression turned serious as he added, "It's been a long time since Simone."

I swallowed the pang of pain. "I know. My other problem is I get the feeling she can see that I'm lying through my teeth."

Rhodes appeared in the doorframe of my bedroom as I pulled out a long-sleeved black sweater. Not too formal, not too casual. Dressed up just enough.

He studied me up and down. "You're a looker, bro. It should be easy."

I still couldn't get used to Rhodes's American accent. He was just as British as I was, but the accent was part of his cover in Los Angeles. The missions he worked on and the government officials he often worked with expected Rhodes Matheson, who was very much an American. Marcus Black was British, which at least made my life easier. It was one thing to use an accent for a mission, maybe a day or two. But to live fully American, that was brutal.

Rhodes was engaged, but his fiancée didn't seem to notice that everything wasn't quite as it seemed. We were all pretenders.

"Just remember, you need to be a gentleman, bro."

I scowled. "I *am* a gentleman."

"No, a gentleman eats, sleeps, and *fucks*. You, Marcus, are a soldier. For you, it's eat, sleep, mission. No fucking. No smoothing the rough edges. You have to change your mindset. Release the pressure valve."

I was smooth, damn it. "Fine. I'll smooth the edges." I *had* been a little twitchy lately.

"I'm telling you, bro, it'll be a lot easier."

I sighed. "Can you go now? You're going to make me late."

"Do you have condoms?"

I pointed at the door. "Out."

He chuckled. "I'm gonna take this beer with me."

"Jesus fucking Christ, Rhodes, you can't drink and drive here."

"I'm walking." He winked.

"Pretty sure there's an ordinance against having an open container too."

He shrugged and then turned up the beer bottle, chugging the full contents.

He dangled the empty bottle in front of me. "Happy now?"

"Yeah, fine. Go."

He nodded, touched me on the shoulder as a conveyance of good luck, and walked out the door. Then I was off to meet Lyra.

She'd told me she'd be coming from work, so I had picked a place between our flat and her office. She worked at this marketing and PR company in downtown Culver City that was ten blocks away from our building. Most days I watched her as she'd take her route to work. Sometimes she would drive, not often though. Occasionally she would detour and go the other way. Not that I paid *that* much attention to her.

Sure, you don't.

I'd only been sitting outside the bistro for three minutes when Lyra rounded the corner. The white flared skirt she wore flirted and skimmed her thighs with every step. She carried some kind of printed orange, pink and yellow clutch. Her fuchsia wrap top lifted her breasts high enough to tease and make my mouth water. The V of her top along with the strip of belly showing tempted my brain into all kinds of inventive lasciviousness. But I worked hard to keep my gaze on her and not the mouthwatering glimpses of deep brown skin.

Christ, she looked good enough to eat.

More like devour.

When she saw me, she gave me a wave, and I watched as she inhaled deeply and then let out a long breath. Then her smile broadened as she started across the street. Nerves?

Something tripped over my skin when she was mere steps away. It was like the breeze wafted her lime and coconut shampoo my way. Bloody hell, she smelled good. She always had. I only wished I was the shag she wanted, but then Rhodes's impromptu pep talk reminded me that there was more at stake than just wanting to shag a pretty girl. If the boss was aware of me not toeing the company line, there would be hell to pay, and I didn't want that.

I liked a quiet life where I could focus on my career.

You mean where you can hide.

I was going to need to sort this out.

When she reached me, she extended her arms, and I stood and gave her a hug. In moments like that, when I was touching her, when she was close and I could smell her scent wrapped around me like a boa constrictor claiming me as her own, I felt like *hell fucking yes, I can do this whole relationship thing.* Her softness was something that called to me. Made a part of my brain believe this could be real.

Then she stepped back, giving me a perfunctory kiss on the cheek, and that was it. As the scent of coconut and lime teased me, my gaze focused on her full, very bitable lips. How was it we hadn't even kissed yet?

How was it I hadn't licked into her mouth and found out all her secrets? How was it I'd never heard her moan?

Fuck. I swallowed hard. I was going to have to think about that because the way I wanted to kiss her might lead to some loss of control. "Hey, you're looking well."

Her smile was bright. "You too. You look good in black. You feeling better?"

I frowned, then forced my expression to relax as I remembered my food poisoning cover story. "Much. Maybe we'll actually get to finish this date."

She laughed at that. "Please, don't jinx it."

When the conversation was surface topics, things were easy. Relaxed. Familiar. Like I could do this with her. But once we sat down and I asked about her work, I felt like I was getting a presentation. Like the woman whom I wanted to get to know, the one with the knockout scent who harnessed the sun in her smile, took a backseat and was replaced by a completely different woman. One who, while perfectly *nice*— engaging even—was not *real* somehow. Maybe I was projecting. Because hell, *I* wasn't real. I was a bloody Tin Man.

And then, of course, she said, "How is work going? You are designing your own game, right?"

I knew exactly which Marcus suit to access. We got briefs weekly with work notes to memorize so we could better play real people. "It's great. I ran into some difficulties, but in the end, I got it working. It's boring, I know."

"No," she said enthusiastically. "It's not boring at all. I want to hear about what you do."

The irony of it was that, if push came to shove, I could probably put some sort of game together. I'd been trained in the field. I had a photographic memory. It wasn't super complex, but I didn't actually *do* the job, so it made lying about it difficult.

"You were telling me that your brother had a baby. A son, right?"

I sighed. "A baby boy." Liam had a girl. Using real details was encouraged, but just bits and pieces of them. We were trained to keep things similar but blurred.

Once dessert was served, my heart started to beat faster. It was time that we figured out if we were going to keep doing this. I liked her, but would it be awkward if we just stopped?

Would it be awkward for you? Find something you like about this woman. Make it stick.

After I paid the check and we left the restaurant, I took her hand.

It was the quickest movement, but her gaze flickered down to our joined hands. The smile she gave me was bright, warm, inviting. But her eyes were wary. Searching.

Did she find what she was looking for? Most people would have believed the façade, but not Lyra. If I knew what was good for me, I would pick someone else. Someone easier. There was nothing easy about Lyra. She was looking for the *real* me, but she wasn't going to find it. That would be dangerous for the both of us.

But still, she let me hold her hand and comfortably fit her small, delicate one in mine. The electric hum that snaked up my arm was almost impossible to ignore. The more time I spent with her, the more I wanted her.

When we reached the community garden in the park near our building, I stopped her. "So I've been thinking. It's the third date." I watched her visibly swallow, hard.

"I'm sorry. I'm really nervous."

That moment of realness made me grin. "There's probably no need to be nervous."

Her brows lifted, and then she blinked rapidly in surprise. "Oh, right, yeah. Sure, totally. We can just be friends."

Friends? I shook my head. For some reason, I had an aversion to that idea. "No, I meant before we—you know, get nervous about anything *else*, maybe we should kiss first?"

She choked out a laugh. "Oh my God, I'm like the worst date ever. I'm all stiff and awkward, then I proposition you."

I laughed. "No. We've been busy and then on our first date, you got called for a work emergency."

She winced. "I'm really sorry about that. And well, you were sick the next time."

Right... sick. "We could try it now." My voice sounded like someone had put it through a cement mixer.

You've been staring at her lips all through dinner, wondering if one kiss will tell you how this is supposed to go.

The community garden was helping me out with ambiance. It had tea lights strung around the trees inside. I'd helped with planting some of the flowers earlier in the year, and they had all started to bloom now. It was the perfect romantic spot for a kiss.

"Oh, right, yeah. L-let's do this."

There was something endearing about her. She was tiny compared to me. Five foot six or seven. I couldn't tell properly because she was almost always wearing heels. Either way, I towered over her. I stood six foot three, so I had a tendency to do that to everyone. She was lean, slender but curvy. Great arse. The kind you could really dig your hands into.

And slap.

I cleared my throat to erase that mental imagery. Nope. I would not think about slapping her arse. I would not think about her arse at all. This was just a kiss.

I would kiss her and see if she was okay with that. And then later—much later—I'd think about slapping her arse. Maybe doing *other things* to her arse, but that was beside the point.

She stepped in, her scent making me dizzy, coaxing me to lean in, get a whiff, and become ensnared in her trap forever. I took her arm, sliding my fingers along her soft, supple skin until my thumb reached her wrist and paused at the pulse point. I could feel the uptake as I gently rubbed that spot. Something stirred deep inside me as an answer to that rapid flutter. And then her other arm wrapped around my neck and she whispered, "Okay, Marcus Black, let's see what you've got."

I grinned then, and holy shit, as I leaned down and she leaned up, the scent of her, the feel of her against me, caused everything else to fade away. Black out our surroundings. Just fade to black.

She tasted sweet, like the plum cocktail she'd had at dinner. But there was something else. A hint of spice that was all her. When her tongue met mine, I stopped thinking and let the tingling, snapping heat fry my synapses. Her lips were soft and yielding. Then she whimpered, and all the blood went straight to my dick.

The hairs at the back of my neck stood at attention. And every instinct I had in me told me to take cover. Everything in me told me this was dangerous. That *she* was dangerous. And suddenly, we were knocked off our feet.

Literally.

I protected her with my body as we both toppled over.

Tackled.

I quickly cradled her head as I rolled over her, reaching for my ankle holster before I remembered I was out in public with a woman who didn't know I carried a gun.

Pulling back, I assessed her quietly. "Look at me. Are you okay?"

Her eyes were wide, and she looked like she needed a moment to recover. "Son of a bitch. He just took my purse."

And before I could stop her, she jumped up and took off sprinting after the mugger in the darkened park with her stilettos in hand.

Well, hell.

2

MARCUS

F*uck me.* She was fast.

I'd never seen her running. Maybe she used the treadmill in the gym?

I never ran into her there. Nor had I noticed her coming back from a workout.

You need to cool it with the stalking. That shit is just creepy.

I wasn't being a creep. I was just aware of movements in the building. It was part of my training. Maybe she had a treadmill in her flat, which was entirely possible.

When I finally caught up with them, she'd almost caught up with the assailant, and she wound her arm back and tossed her shoes at him. Her aim was strikingly accurate, and one of the stilettos spiked right into his upper thigh.

With a grimace, he pulled out the shoe then tried to run again. She stayed on him, but I stopped her with a hand on her arm and I went after the mugger instead. After a brief sprint through the tomato plots, I caught him easily, whipping him around and wrapping an arm around his neck and securing it with my other arm. Lyra was right beside me as I dragged off his mask.

My gaze roamed over his face. The lower half was familiar, but what I really noted was the tattoo on his wrist. *Victus.* An Eastern European gang with links to terrorism. What the fuck was he doing here in Los Angeles?

With one hand, I tried to keep her back, lest he grab for her, because then all bets were off. "Let me handle this."

Oh sure, the video game designer knows how to interrogate someone?

Fucking hell. If I let him go, he might hurt her. I knew his gang well. They were vicious. Ruthless. Deadly.

She reached for her bag in his hand, ignoring my attempts to keep her out of reach, but he didn't let it go. "You stole that from me, you dickwad."

Dickwad? My lips twitched. Because I was more occupied with trying to get her out of the way so I could get her to safety, I missed the punch coming. It didn't hurt, but it was surprising.

That was the problem with women. *Distractions.*

Then she squeaked at me. "Jesus, are you okay?"

I noticed one thing though; she was still holding onto her purse and trying to wrestle it away from him.

"Lyra, let him have it."

"Like hell I will. This is an HD Accra original."

Was she serious? "A what now?"

The would-be mugger was fighting her for it, but Lyra wasn't letting go.

I tried to get between them, but she wasn't having it. And then in the scuffle, Lyra finally managed to get her purse free, *after* she kneed the bloke in the groin.

He went down like a sack, clutching his mangled balls and groaning.

The sudden release of pressure on her bag also caused Lyra to stumble backward and go down. With a quick glance at her, I asked, "Are you okay?"

She was on all fours then, wincing. "I think I scraped my knee, but I'm fine."

Turning my full attention back to the Victus idiot, I reached for him and hauled him up. "You're going to die," I whispered in his ear, low enough to convey the proper amount of menace and instill the right dosage of fear but not have *her* hear me.

I was aware that I only had one option, given the scenario. The police. In which case, this idiot would either die in lock up, or whoever had brought him here would bail him out before I could get to him.

But *he* knew there was another option. One where I'd been so worried about Lyra that I'd failed to pat him down to check for weapons. The deafening click of a safety being released made me freeze as he asked, "Are you sure about that?"

I swallowed hard as I released him and put my hands up. I backed up slowly, careful to put myself between the gun and Lyra. "What do you want?"

"Soon you'll see." Then he grabbed Lyra's purse and ran, leaving the two of us to stare after him.

What I wanted to do was chase him. Find him. Kill him slowly. There were so many ways I could entertain killing him.

I didn't know who he was, and I didn't care. I'd find out why he'd come for me eventually. But I had to get Lyra to safety first.

Kneeling down next to her, I helped her to her feet. I could feel her shaking, so I wrapped my arms around her and held her close. "I'm so sorry. Are you okay?"

She gave me a vigorous nod. "I know I shouldn't have gone after him, but my mom gave that purse to me. And you almost died because of it."

I frowned. Her mother was dead. She'd never told me that, but I knew it from my background check on her. But I couldn't question her about it now. All I could do was rub her back and try to comfort her. "I'm so sorry, Lyra."

She nodded. "She passed away when I was eighteen."

I winced. "That's rough."

"Thanks. I just—I don't know. I couldn't just let him have it." She glared toward the direction he'd run like she wanted to go after him and knee him in the nuts all over again.

I nodded. "It was a part of you. I'm just glad you're not seriously hurt. Let's get you home and call the police."

She wobbled on her feet. "The police?"

Not my idea of fun either, love. But that was the thing normal people would do, and I had to maintain my cover above all else. I'd worry about Victus later. "We were mugged, Lyra. We need the police. They handle things like this."

"Right, of course. Sorry, I just feel a little foggy."

I wrapped an arm around her and led her out of the garden and back toward our apartment building. "Are you sure you're not seriously hurt?"

"Nothing a little topical biotin won't solve." Even though her voice was steady, her brow was furrowed in concentration or pain. I wasn't sure which.

I glanced down and saw that her knee was bloody with thick red rivulets running down her leg. "Jesus, Lyra." I reached down, but she scooted away from me.

"Oh my God. I—I'm fine. I would do a lot worse falling off a treadmill."

I frowned. After watching her run, I could never see her falling off of anything. "You strike me as quite graceful."

"Oh yeah, what part of that fall was graceful?"

"You took down the assailant with a knee to the balls, which was well played, I have to say."

"But did you see me falling in the process?"

"I'll show you how to do that, so you don't lose your balance."

She lifted her brows. "You took a punch, too."

I waved her off. "Stop it. I have a brother. I barely felt that."

"I'd love to travel to London one day and meet your brother."

Yes, travel was on her list of things she'd always wanted to do but never seemed to have time for. That phrasing always irritated me, because when people really wanted to do something, they somehow managed to find a way to do it. Not Lyra, though. "Well, I offer to be your tour guide."

"That would be really fun. Guaranteed to be more fun than getting mugged on a date."

When we reached our building, instead of walking her to her door, I led her to mine. The designers of the building had a quirky design aesthetic. None of the numbers were sequential. And none of the doors matched. Every single one was designed for uniqueness and individuality. "Let's call the police from my place and we'll get you cleaned up. Besides, he has your wallet, so I'd love to get the police at least watching your place before you go home."

She hesitated.

All I wanted to do was get her behind the titanium plating

of my door to protect her, but obviously she thought I wanted something else.

I wanted her, but now wasn't the time. I didn't want to scare her away though. I wasn't going to give her a chance to entertain that thought now that I'd detected some actual spunk in her. Tonight she'd been on fire.

The things you find sexy are ridiculous.

"Come on. Let's go in."

Her eyes went wide. "Um, Marcus, I-I think you're great. I just, uh—"

I spoke slowly. "I just want to take care of your knee. Eventually, I do want to continue that kiss, but you know... at some point when you aren't bleeding all over yourself."

She blinked rapidly. "Oh. It's fine, honestly. I'm just going to clean it up and take a shower—"

"Right. But it's a lot easier when someone else does it for you."

"No, you don't really need to—"

I pushed open the door and waited for her to enter before following.

She sighed. "Okay, then. I appreciate the knight-in-shining-armor duty, I do, but this is completely unnecessary."

"Let me decide what's unnecessary, would you?" I led her down the hall to my loo. I knew my loft was a mirror image of hers. "Come on in here. It will be easier to clean up, and you won't get blood anywhere."

"I'm not bleeding that bad."

With every step, she left a few drops of blood. I hoped she didn't need stiches. "Yes, you are."

She glanced down at her knee and winced. "Ugh. No more skirts for a while then."

"Don't worry, with a little vitamin E oil, your legs will still look amazing."

Her gaze flickered up to meet mine. "Oh, you think my legs look amazing?"

I grinned then. "Your legs *are* amazing, but you know that already."

"Do I?"

I cocked my head up. "You've never struck me as one who needs flattery."

"I am still a woman."

I chuckled. "I had noted."

Her whole demeanor had changed. Her cheeks were flushed. Her eyes were a little wide. She looked energized. Invigorated. Sexy.

"Hop up here." I patted the counter, and she frowned.

"You know I can do this myself."

"Yes, but I can also do it for you. And wouldn't that be nice?"

She blinked up at me and then gave me a nod. "Okay, bossy."

"You're not the first person to tell me that."

"No? Are you always this bossy, and why haven't I ever noticed it before?"

"I never had an occasion to boss you around before. But if you like to be bossed around, I can manage that."

Her nose scrunched, and I wanted to press a kiss to the gently wrinkled skin. "I don't usually like it."

I cocked my head and stared at her. "Well, if you ever need someone bossy, I'm open for hire."

She laughed. "Thanks. I'll remember that."

It struck me how easily I could be this person. Flirt with her.

Be this other version of me. I gently cleaned the scrapes on her knee. I was amazed at her ability to withstand pain, because most people I knew would be screaming their bloody heads off. She just merely looked on, wincing once or twice. When she was all clean, I took her hands and cleaned those off too.

"Honestly, this is overkill."

"You keep saying that. And I keep telling you that it's not."

She winced. "I probably should not have chased that idiot."

"It was really brave though."

"Well, my aunt calls me impetuous. Always diving in headfirst."

"You get mugged often?"

She laughed. "No, thank God."

"Well, we survived."

"Thank you for the doctoring," she said hurriedly.

"That's okay. I told you it's better if someone else does it. Don't you agree?"

"Sure, I guess. Well, thanks for everything."

I lifted my brow. She wanted to be rid of me. Why was that?

"Lyra?"

"Hmm?"

"I'm getting the impression that you want to be rid of me. Tell me I'm wrong."

Lyra

HE WASN'T WRONG. I did want to be rid of him.

Because I wanted to go kick some ass. Stannis Prochenko's ass to be specific. I'd recognized him immediately when Marcus tore off his mask. What was he doing in LA? Why was he after me? That son of a bitch had taken my purse, but for what reason? The ID was fake. The address was fake. It led to a bait house in Koreatown, but Marcus didn't know that. He'd been very heroic, but I knew he was lucky to still be alive.

He'd had no idea who he was trying to protect me from.

I was surprised, actually. He'd been remarkably capable. Fast. Well-conditioned. And the wrestling move he'd used to get Stannis in the chokehold was impressive.

But as capable as he was, he was no match for Stannis.

Besides, Stannis was my kill.

Easy does it. You can't kill every idiot who comes for you.

Under normal circumstances, I would have let a random mugger go. But there was a gun in my purse. The last thing I needed was for some idiot to find the gun and use it. It was untraceable with the serial number filed off, but still, I didn't want to be part of him killing someone with a gun he'd stolen from me. So I'd had to go after him. And then, of course, Marcus Black stepped in with his stupid sexy shoulders and uncanny way of dealing with the mugger.

Since when do you think his shoulders are sexy?

I frowned at that. Something had happened in that fight. He'd just taken that hit to the jaw that would have crumpled half the agents I knew. I supposed he was lucky and hadn't taken the brunt of it. He'd been paying attention to me, worrying about my safety.

How was I supposed to tell him I was the last person on earth that he should be worried about? I was more than capable. And it's not like I didn't have a knife strapped to my thigh. Honestly, I could have dispatched that idiot Prochenko in seconds.

But Captain America over there had wanted to do the right thing. But now, if he would just let me leave, I could go after that idiot.

I scowled. There was a part of me that thought maybe the mugging had been something untoward, something other than what it was. But what if it had just been an ordinary mugging? They happened all the time. We lived in the States, for the love of Christ. Still though, it was harder to just accept that idea knowing who it was. I wanted to go out and find him. Remind him why it wasn't nice to take things that didn't belong to him.

That is vengeance. We don't do vengeance.

Marcus was speaking. His voice was lower than I'd ever heard it before. There was something sexier about him that night. And God, was that stubble? He was always so clean shaven, looking extra Boy Scout-like. I didn't like a mountain man beard, but a little five-o'clock shadow? That was hot. What else was different about him?

"Hmm?"

"I was saying it seems like you were trying to get rid of me."

"I'm not. But I think you've done enough for one evening. You were my knight in shining armor. I don't want to take up any more of your time."

"Ah, the brush-off."

I sighed. He was very cute. So good looking. But if I was being honest, he was a complication. And I didn't need complications.

"Marcus, I like you. You are—well, you know what you look like."

"I think I would probably like it more if you told me."

I grinned at that. When had he gotten so... I don't know... sexy?

Maybe that was the adrenaline talking. Or was it because I watched him pick up that mugger by his shirt like it was nothing? His shoulders had bunched, and he was decidedly less nice. Was that it? Just a hint that there was something under the façade, and suddenly my blood was boiling?

"You're great, Marcus. Honestly, you are. But maybe I'm just not ready to date right now."

"Uh-huh," he said.

"I just got out of a thing a while ago." I used a line that I'd built my profile with on the site. "Maybe I just need more time."

"Uh-huh."

"And thank you. Did I ever say thank you? You saved me. I just—" My gaze flickered to his lips.

"You think we should be friends?"

I nodded. "Yes, friends. *Friends* sounds good."

He could be my friend.

Except none of your friends have shoulders like that.

"Lyra?"

I lifted my head, blinking and hoping I was giving him a demure *I'm not trying to run out on you* look. I just wanted to leave so I could go chase that whacked-up mugger.

"I have enough friends. I'm not really looking for any more."

I frowned at that. I didn't want him to disappear; I just didn't need any sudden complications.

Maybe you don't like that tingle low in your belly that you haven't felt in practically forever.

"Right. So, can we just—"

"Lyra?"

"Yeah."

"You keep looking at me like I'm dinner."

And then I kissed him. A tingling buzz and hum drifted over my skin, making me alert in the kind of way that worried me. I'd never felt that before. I'd been kissed of course, usually on jobs or for practice. So I'd only kissed marks and other operators, but nothing had ever felt like this.

His lips were a slow, silken caress and a complete surprise. One I hadn't been prepared for. I gasped into his mouth, and all that gentleness, all that tentativeness was gone. He deepened the kiss. Not pushing me. More like coaxing me. His tongue delved in, and I caught a spear of need into the center of my core. I tried to clamp my legs together, but since he was standing in front of me where I sat on the bathroom counter, all they did was clamp around his hips. He groaned and then cupped both of my cheeks in his hands and angled my head just how he needed it to stroke his tongue against mine, making me want things I had never needed. Sure, I had *wanted*, but I had never *needed* before. Holy hell. Where had this man been hiding?

A tingling need unfurled low in my belly, turning into a wildfire, then an inferno. He changed the angle and the pressure again, teasing me into playing, into being part of the game. Taking the dare, my tongue slid over his, falling into his mouth, exploring tentatively but ready to run. But the spell he wove around me made it impossible to run because I wanted him more than I had ever wanted anything.

And then the alarm bells rang in my head.

Too close, Lyra. Too close to danger. Back down.

I retreated, and he let me, the kiss slowing as I drew back slightly.

He cleared his throat. "See, I don't think we're friends." And then he backed away. "I know you said you wanted to shower, so I will walk you home. When the police get here, I'll give them a statement and arrange for you to give them one in the morning."

I was in a daze, my lips still tingling from his kiss when he dropped me in front of my apartment. "Thank for everything."

His lips tipped up into a smirk. "You're welcome. And so you know, since our date was interrupted again, we'll be getting a re-do."

He leaned against the wall as he made sure I went in.

"Goodnight, Lyra. Let me know when you're up for the do-over."

All I could do was stare at his back as he stomped down the hall like he owned the place. Who the hell was Marcus Black? And had he awakened a monster?

3

MARCUS

H oly shit.

Kissing Lyra Wilkinson was like sticking my whole body in an electrical socket. The buzzing hum stayed with me as I walked back to my flat.

I locked the door behind me, then double locked it and chained it because I wanted to make it difficult for myself when my body prompted me to go back and finish that kiss. Finish it naked. Finish it with her screaming my name.

What the hell? Where had that side of the woman been hiding? She kissed like she was discovering kissing for the first time and really, really liked it.

How had I not seen it before? I ran my hands through my hair and paced in an attempt to burn off some of the energy.

You were too in your head. Now enjoy it.

Fucking hell. She was dangerous

I needed a clear head. She'd tried to give me that 'we should be friends' nonsense.

Friends? What kind of shite was that?

She wanted to walk away. That had never happened

before. Whenever I put my mind into something or someone, they all wanted to stay. But not Lyra. I might have let her go if she hadn't kissed me.

We needed to stop with this banal small talk and start touching more. There should be *lots* more touching. I'd seen her tonight, the *real* her, not the version she presented to the world. She was like me. Well, she was normal. But normal or not, there was a part of her she kept safe, hidden.

I wanted to know about her life. But all those important things that I had found in my background search, she hadn't told me any of it. Nada. It was as if she had parts of her that she was willing to share, but I hadn't passed muster, so I didn't get to hear it. Which was bullshit.

Lyra and I would deal with each other later. I had more pressing questions. I lifted one of the cushions in my couch and then adjusted the tab until it stayed up and revealed the keypad beneath it. A couple of quick taps, and I was able to log in. Curtis, my handler, answered. "Marcus, it's Friday night. What's the matter?"

"I was mugged today."

Curtis cursed. "You should have called housekeeping."

I grunted. "No, he's still alive."

There was a beat of silence. "What?"

"I was on a date. We got mugged by a member of Victus. I couldn't deal with him in front of a civilian. Advise."

He cursed. "Where were you?"

I gave him the pertinent details, and he was silent as he waited for me to finish. He knew if I was calling it in, something important and immediate needed to be done. The team had learned to trust my instincts. "Is my cover at risk?"

"No. You're clean. There is no chatter on you or your ID."

"You want me to believe it was a coincidence? No way.

There was something about the way it happened. Like he was waiting for us. I don't know. It just feels wrong."

Curtis was quiet for a moment. "Victus has all sorts of low-level minions. No need for alarm yet. Have you involved law enforcement?"

"No. But that will be the expectation since I was with a civilian," I muttered. The police were just going to make this messy.

"We'll send a team in."

"Fine. In the meantime, get me what you have on Victus operatives working in the States. They've never had a presence here, so why now?"

"Is the civilian able to compromise you?"

I froze. I knew what he was asking. He wanted to know if Lyra had seen me do anything out of the ordinary. Something they'd have to make her forget. "No. It was a run of the mill date. But he took her purse, so have the team ask her about it when they question her."

Curtis sighed. "Fine. Likely he's a contractor passing through just getting his kicks with a little light robbery. The civilian, you vetted her?"

Shit. "Yes. I used Hans." Hans was our resident hacker. There wasn't a system he couldn't break. Other than thinking Lyra was hot, he'd found nothing remotely interesting about her.

"Fine. Come in for a debrief tomorrow, and we'll send a team to interview the civilian."

"One more thing, Curtis. He managed to hit me. He could have killed me, but he didn't."

Curtis's voice went icier. "That sounds personal, Marcus."

"It's never personal. I don't know him. He did hurt my friend though."

Curtis was silent for a beat. "Your friend? The civilian?"

"Yes."

"Control will be happy that you're heeding their advice." I could hear both surprise and pleasure in the tone of his voice.

"Well, I'm not doing it for Control. The point is, she's a nice, normal woman."

"Oh, sounds *exciting*. Aren't you glad you had that date?"

I laughed. "Actually, I am."

Curtis's chuckle was low. "If you say so. I'll check on what you need to do and get back to you."

Maybe I was overreacting, but something was off. I didn't know what it was, but I could feel it in my bones. I pulled up the surveillance on my front hall and kept the cameras trained on Lyra's flat.

She wasn't mine. I knew that. At the same time, I couldn't help that suspicious feeling. Like she needed my protection.

Are you sure that's not just you getting attached?

No, I wasn't getting attached. Being with her would take care of one of my problems. Control would finally get off my arse now. That whole *attachments look normal, let us control your life* thing. I had zero interest in that.

What I did have an interest in was Lyra Wilkinson. And tonight she'd finally shown me a part of herself. Something real. And that real part of her was impossible to resist. And just in case I was right about the mugger targeting me, I needed to keep her safe. Because she had no idea who I was.

And that made her a target too.

You'll be repeating history.

Lyra

IF I WAS BEING ENTIRELY honest with myself, I wasn't sure how long I sat there against my door with my bandaged knee that had been kissed all better by Marcus Black. But eventually, I found my brain cells.

They'd been drugged by Marcus and his kisses, but they were in full functioning order again. I stood slowly, wincing slightly as my knee smarted. Son of a bitch. That little shit Prochenko really did need a lesson taught to him.

Stop being impetuous.

I could practically hear Roz in my head. But this wasn't about me being impetuous. Stannis was here. And he was here for a reason. Not to mention that now he was armed with *my* gun.

I marched into the bathroom, carefully tugged a shower cap over my hair, then took a quick, perfunctory shower, wincing as the water and soap sluiced over my knee.

When I was done, I let my hair out of the strategic bobby pins I'd used to pile all the curls to one side. I wrapped myself in a robe and then went to my bookshelf. I'd been so happy when I moved in here. Roz had set it up for me, just how I loved it. Books galore with a fantastic hidden compartment.

I pulled my copy of *Pride and Prejudice* down to a forty-five-degree angle. On the inside panel of the book was a keypad on which I tapped in my code, and voilà; the shelves split apart, revealing my weapons arsenal as well as a communications portal.

I never left the house without a weapon. Though tonight, that practice had bit me in the ass. And not in a fun, dirty kind of way I wanted from Marcus.

What do you know about dirty?

I knew things. I'd read a lot. I might not have a whole ton of practical experience, but I did like dirty books. Maybe Marcus Black would be willing to try practical dirty application.

I rolled my eyes at myself. One kiss and my body was ready to jump on that Marcus Black train and ride it for all it was worth. I needed help.

Inside my little weapons vault, there was a secure computer to check in with work. I did a quick check to make sure that Addie hadn't been sent out on a mission while I was on my date. And when I saw that she was in, on site for the night, I called her secure line.

She answered with, "Home already? That's really disappointing, Lyra."

"Hey," I muttered petulantly. "Who said it was disappointing?"

"Honey, it's not even midnight."

"So?" Okay, yes. That was sad.

"Are you calling me with him in your apartment?"

I sighed. I could almost picture her. Blond curls cascading around her shoulders, bright topaz-colored eyes narrowed in a shrewd expression as she tried to ascertain the truth in something. She knew me.

"Okay, to be fair, it's not my fault the date ended early."

She laughed. "Uh-huh. Of course, it's not your fault, baby."

"It's not," I insisted. "I got mugged."

She went deadly serious then. "Is that why you're calling? Were there witnesses? Do I need to engage Babel Protocol?"

Why did everyone always assume I handled things with my weapons? You accidentally stab one human trafficker, and no one ever let you forget it. "No need for Babel. He's still standing. I had no choice. I was with a witness."

"That sounds more like it."

"One more thing. I knew the mugger. It was Stannis Prochenko."

That name alone made Addie put on her serious voice. "Did he follow you? Does he know where you live?"

"Undetermined. He interrupted my date, but there were no indications he followed us home."

"Did your date see him? Would he be able to identify Stannis?"

I had no time to think, but my brain did the processing for me. If at any point The Firm thought we had exposure from Marcus they might decide to deal with him. So I did the only thing I could. I lied. "No. I ran after him. I saw him as I was trying to get his mask off but when the civilian approached, I put the mask back. I didn't want him having exposure." Over the years I'd learned to lie expertly. But I'd never lied to Addie. It didn't sit well to do it now.

"Jesus Ly, that could have been bad."

"I know." I rubbed my temples in an attempt to ward off the adrenaline headache. "I want an assessment on my ID and location."

She sighed. "Only you would somehow get mugged by a member of Victus on a date."

"I didn't go *looking* for any trouble. Trouble found me."

"Jesus, Ly."

"You know what? You say that like this is my fault. I was standing there, minding my business and looking cute and kissing a hot guy, who by the way, is an *excellent* kisser, and bam, we got tackled."

There was another beat of silence. "Uh, I need you to rewind to that part about kissing a hottie."

I smirked at that. "Oh, you caught that, did you?"

"Did you and Mr. Boring finally knock boots?"

"No, we did not knock boots. But we did kiss, and he's been holding back on me." Her giddy squeal made me laugh, and I chuckled. "No getting excited."

"Who's getting excited? I'm just saying it's about time he dusted off your vag."

"I don't want my vag to be dusted off, Addie. Can we focus on the mugger, please?"

"Oh my God, fine. I'll take a look. Now, tell me everything."

"We were about to really, really make that kiss worth something, and then the mugging happened. The guy grabbed my purse and I chased him down."

She sighed. "Lyra."

"What? My gun was inside the bag."

"What's one gun on the street? There are millions. Sad but true. It's untraceable."

"You know I can't let that fly, Addie."

She sighed. "Do-gooder Lyra. I do love you for it."

"You are a do-gooder too, Addie."

"No, I'm not. I just play one on ops."

"Stop it. You're very good at your job."

"I am, but sometimes I wish I wasn't so good at it. But anyway, I've got an eye out. If anything comes up, we'll see it."

"Thanks. It was my favorite gun."

"You and that damn gun." She rolled her eyes.

Roz had given it to me when I first joined The Firm. It was a small, compact Beretta. I disliked the fact that it was a girl gun, but I did like that it fit in my bag.

I felt a pang when I thought of that purse. My mother had

been a fashion designer. I'd travelled with her a lot when I was a kid for her work. That purse had been part of her collection. When I was seventeen, I'd borrowed it without permission and gotten an ink stain on the inner lining.

My mother had been less than pleased and banned me from ever borrowing it again. But at my graduation from high school, she'd relented and let me borrow it. And when she died, she left me everything. But like the rest of my old life, I'd buried that part of me in a storage facility near where I'd grown up outside of Boston.

The HD Accra had been the only item I'd kept with me in my new life.

It was funny how buried memories never wanted to stay that way.

Most of the things, I'd doled out to my aunts. I'd only kept the HD Accra clutch. The son of a bitch had taken it from me, so I wanted access to him to make him pay.

We're not in the revenge business.

Yes, yes, not in the revenge business. Blah-blah-blah.

"Hey, we all have our crutches."

Addie turned the topic back toward what she wanted to hear. "So back to this mind-blowing kiss. And please, *please* tell me you saw a dick."

"No, I did not. But I sure felt one though."

"Okay, this is getting better."

I laughed. "Oh Addie, no, he, um, helped clean my knee because I got hurt."

Addie laughed. "Did you even feel the skinned knee?"

"No. But still, I had to pretend and play it up for him."

She chuckled softly. "If he only had a clue about our training."

"The skinned knee was hardly something to even stop for.

Anyway, he cleaned up my cuts, patched me up and all that goodness, and then I tried to let him down easy."

She groaned. "Oh my God, no. Why?"

"Well, you know, I just... If I have trouble, I'm not dropping it at his doorstep. That's not fair."

"Right. Okay, then what?"

"Then I tried to tell him that we were probably great as friends. He said he had zero interest in that because he had plenty of friends. And then I kissed him."

All I heard was a slapping noise from her end. "Hot damn. Yes, you did. Way to send mixed messages."

I snorted a laugh then. "You're ridiculous. I was confused, okay?"

"I know. But that's why I'm so loveable. Anyway, so you kissed, and then?"

My insides warmed just thinking about the slow slide of his tongue and the way his hands fisted ever so slightly in my hair. "It was a really, *really* good kiss."

She cackled at that. "About damn time. Now do you see what you've been missing out on? Hooking up with Valentine ops, while handy, is not the way to do things. It makes it so much hotter if you're like totally into the guy."

My skin prickled. Addie was the only person other than Roz who knew what had happened with Tyler. I was twenty-one, and Roz had been training me for two years. I had the makings of a great agent, but I still froze on any operation that required me to cozy up to men.

It wasn't that I was uncomfortable; it was more that I didn't really know my body. I hadn't had much opportunity to date, and before I knew it, I was an agent. So Roz had introduced me to Tyler. His job was to show me the ropes, teach me how to flirt and kiss. At no point was it supposed to turn into anything real, but nobody told *me* that. So I'd believed the stolen kisses, the whispered words. I'd believed that high, lightheaded, freefall feeling. After all, Tyler was very good at his job.

For four months, he treated me like his girlfriend. When neither one of us was out on a mission, we were together. Tooled around town like a couple. Shopping and movie nights and bowling. And then one day, he dropped me. Wouldn't take my calls, didn't even say hello to me in the halls. He was cold and perfunctory. I didn't handle it well. Matter of fact, I demanded that he tell me what the hell was going on. And ever so helpful as he was, he told me everything.

It had never been real. The Firm had determined that I needed to lose my virginity to be more effective in the field. And he was just the agent that had landed the job.

I'd been *a job*.

Roz had thought that she was doing me some great favor by finding me someone nice, cute, gentle, and kind. Little did she know that his directive was to break me in and then turn me into an effective agent.

I'd never forgiven myself for believing. Then I never got over it. I'd known that in our line of work, lying was par for the course. I'd known better than to trust anyone with a smile and some kind words. But Tyler... He really, *truly* cemented that distrust. And something icy and cold had wrapped around my heart.

And now I realized that for all his expertise, that floaty feeling of first discovery, I'd still never felt with him the way that I had when Marcus kissed me. Like I was being struck by little tiny lightning bolts all over my body. Like all I wanted to do was rub my body all against him. Like I was willing to beg for whatever he might give me.

Not that I was going to beg, because I refused to ever be that pathetic again. It was for the best that Marcus Black and I stayed away from each other.

After everything was over, I finally confessed everything about Tyler to Addie in a drunken night of feeling sorry for myself. I was relieved when Tyler was reassigned to the London office. It wasn't even so much that I still carried a torch for him. It was just that watching my humiliation walk up and down the hallways every day was pure torture.

She laughed. "Good. Oh, Marcus Black, a game builder who can kiss. Will wonders never cease? All right, you, off you get. I'll go see if I can find out what Stannis Prochenko is doing in LA. In the meantime, stay out of trouble. Better yet, call your sexy neighbor. Tell him that you have some pain and he needs to kiss it better."

I furrowed my brow. "I don't have any pain."

She laughed. "You just point to the pain right at your clitoris, and I'm sure he'll make you feel all better."

I choked back a laugh. "Addie."

"What? I'm telling you, he sounds like he's up for the task. Well, I'm glad you had fun. I'll see you tomorrow."

I laughed. "Yeah, okay. Let me know if you find anything."

"Will do."

I hung up with her, unable to shake the feeling of that kiss, the slide of his lips, the stroke of his tongue. I felt like he'd been holding out, like I had to get to know him all over again. This time with kissing.

4

MARCUS

I hadn't slept much. I'd gotten up every hour to double-check the security perimeters and the cameras I had trained on Lyra's flat. No one had come. Nothing had moved. She'd been locked up tight, but I still wasn't comfortable. I wanted to get in her flat and make sure she had proper chains and locks on her doors. I wanted to give her a gun, but she probably would frown on that.

At eight o'clock, I figured it would be safe enough to call Curtis in Hawaii. He answered on the first ring. "You're up early."

"You weren't asleep either."

"I'll sleep when I'm dead."

I chuckled. "Did you find out anything?"

"Yeah. From your description, your would-be mugger is Stannis Prochenko. He was Russian military, then he got caught up in Victus. He's low level though. Not a big player."

I frowned. "Why is that name familiar?"

"Well, you probably know his name in relation to Signat, the terrorist group."

"Yes, that rings a bell. But does that mean Signat or Victus is making a play in the States, and what is he doing in California?"

"Still looking."

"I'm clean though, right. No one even knows I'm here?"

"Yes. I ran your ID several times. There was zero chatter about you. Nothing. He got lucky."

I frowned. "There is no such thing as luck. This is bad."

"Let's not get overexcited. We'll figure it out."

"Anything come back on Lyra Wilkinson?" I knew nothing would, but still, I held my breath.

"No. It's just like you said. She's clean. She had a drunk and disorderly at the funeral home after her parents died, but that's understandable."

"Prochenko might come for her."

"Did she see his face?"

Yes. "No. She was focused on getting her purse back." It was a little lie. One that if I was at headquarters and poly-graphed would make me a concern. But I knew how these things worked. I had to protect her at all costs.

"I have her DMV information. It's for some place in Kore-atown, not her current address."

I blinked in surprise. "So she's safe?"

He sighed. "As far as we know. But if there's a risk for you, we need to call it in and scrub you."

"It's not a risk." I knew what would happen. If I'd been compromised, I would be moved. Sent to some other city. New name, new cover, new lies. It would be as if Marcus Black never existed. And that would leave Lyra a sitting duck. She would have no protection. I tried to reassure him. "No. It's safe. Just double-checking."

Curtis sighed. "You are my most thorough agent. You bend no rules for anyone."

"I know. I'll assess and confirm."

"Let me know if we need housekeeping."

"We *won't* need housekeeping," I said, unable to keep the exasperation out of my voice.

"Mm-hmm. I like to be prepared."

"So do I." I hoped to Christ he'd believe me.

I jumped out of bed and into the shower. Within twenty minutes of my call with Curtis ending, I knocked on Lyra's door.

It was nine o'clock, and I hoped if she was going into work on the weekend that maybe she hadn't left yet.

She answered in her robe and was brushing her teeth. Her eyes went wide when she saw me, and she mumbled, "Hi," around her toothbrush. Then she indicated that she'd be right back and went to the bathroom. When she came back, her face was free of toothpaste suds.

She gave me a curious look. "Ah, is something wrong?"

I shook my head. "No, I just came to check on you."

She blinked, then blinked again, her dark brown eyes searching for something in my gaze. "You didn't have to do that. I'm perfectly fine."

"I know. I figured you'd say that, but I had to see for myself. You had a hell of a scare. Were you able to sleep at all?"

Then she did something I'd never seen her do before. She shuddered. I asked her a simple question, and she shuddered, preparing herself to lie. "Yep. Oh, you know, a couple of bad dreams, but I'm fine. Not the worst thing, I guess."

"Lyra, is that the truth?"

The question was met with more owlish blinking and a raised brow. "What answer are you looking for, Marcus?"

"Just how you are *actually* feeling."

Her brows furrowed, and then she said, "Fine, really. I slept like a baby."

That was the truth. And I wondered how often she'd evaded my questions and I hadn't noticed. But I could tell she wasn't being malicious. There was just a wall, a screen she'd put up between herself and the world. Some kind of deep-seated stuff made her keep herself closed off.

"Okay, good. I was just worried about you because he got your purse."

She blinked at me in surprise. "Oh, uh, it's actually okay. I'm going to get a new license today."

"Yeah, but he has your address."

She winced. "Actually, I never changed it when I moved. I know you're supposed to after thirty days, and it's been a year and a half. But I loved my photo and didn't want a new one."

I chuckled low, tamping down my unease. "Of course. Anyway, at the very least, I wanted to check your locks and see if they're okay."

I turned to the door, and was surprised to see that she had nearly as many locks as I did. "I can't say I'm not happy to see those."

"My dad was kind of a freak about safety, always insisting that we should have the right locks on our doors and windows. I guess I kind of adopted that practice when I got a place of my own."

"Smart of him to do that. And so are you. Still, I'd like you to know I'm here. I can help."

Her smile was warm. "Ah, that's sweet. But honestly, Marcus, you don't have to do that. I can take care of myself."

"I am well aware that you can. I have zero doubts about that. But I'm your neighbor, so you know, I'm just being neighborly."

She laughed then. And I wondered why the hell I had never heard that sound before.

"You already saved my life last night. You didn't need to check on me this morning."

I pulled out the bag I'd gotten from the doughnut place down the street. "If you say so. But surprise! I also brought you breakfast."

She stared at the bag. "You went to Dell's Doughnuts?"

I nodded. "Yes. Because sometimes you need a sugar hit in the morning to get over not sleeping. But since you slept fine, I guess I will just take the doughnuts and go then."

She reached her hands out. "No, hold on just a minute. Who am I to turn down perfectly good doughnuts?"

I laughed. "I knew you'd be a sucker for sugar. Do you have coffee?"

She nodded and then indicated the kitchen. I searched the cupboards until I found plates for the doughnuts.

"So, we're having breakfast together now?" she asked as she joined me at the counter.

I smiled down at her. "Relax, it's just breakfast."

"Right. Are we going to talk about that kiss?"

I smirked at her. "Why? Are you going to try and tell me we should just be friends again?"

Slowly, she shook her head back and forth. "No, but I'm going to tell you that I'm not really dateable. I've got bags and bags of issues, and I'm telling you, you don't want to deal with this."

A powdered sugar dusted the corner of her mouth, and I wanted to lick it right off of her lips. But I settled for using my thumb as I reached over and wiped it off. Her tongue chased my thumb away, and I wanted to feel that sweet flick. She looked up at me and said, "You are dangerous."

I grinned. "Um, no. I'm perfectly safe. I'm not dangerous at all. I'm your next-door neighbor, remember? I program computer games?"

"Yeah, but suddenly there's something very, um... I don't know how to say it. Before last night, you were *different*."

I laughed. "It's the same old me."

"Yeah, but not exactly. I can't quite put my finger on it, but you're different now."

That wasn't good. I didn't want her being quite so astute.

"It's the same me. You're just *seeing* me differently now."

"Is that so?"

I nodded sagely. "We've been in a dating situation together, and now you're starting to notice my muscles."

She snorted then. Full on snort-giggle.

The levity I felt when talking to her was a surprise. Why were things so easy now? "I'm sorry, ma'am, did you just snort?"

She clamped her hand over her mouth quickly. "Oh my God."

I laughed. "No, it's adorable. Really." It was like after I let her see me, even a little bit of myself, it was easier to be around her.

She waved a napkin at me. "Stop it. Don't tease me."

"Trust me, when I'm teasing you, you'll know."

Her eyes went wide and her nostrils flared a little. She cleared her throat, having gotten my meaning. "You'd better go. I have to get ready. I'm going in to work for a few hours."

"Right. Anyway, I really just wanted to bring you breakfast and make sure that you locked up behind you. Having breakfast *with* you was a plus I hadn't planned on, but it was absolutely worth it. And one more thing... Um, do me a favor and get yourself an alarm system or something, okay?"

She blinked at me, owlishly. "I hadn't really thought about it before. You're probably right, though. I should have an alarm system."

"I'm going to call the detective I spoke to last night and just check and see if they have any leads or maybe if they found the guy." Read... My guys in uniforms were going to follow up with her.

"Thank you, Marcus, but I'm sure they have it handled."

I said, "I hear you." But I knew if Stannis Prochenko was coming after her, the police wouldn't be able to stop him. At least not until it was far too late.

Her gaze softened. "You really are a good guy, huh?"

I shrugged. "Sometimes."

Never. You are never the good guy. Good thing she doesn't know who you really are, or she'd run screaming.

And there was no way in hell I was telling her. Prochenko was dangerous. If he sniffed around her at all, she'd end up dead. I'd done this. I brought him to her doorstep, so I needed to fix it.

Or you could stay away. Let them scrub you.

Which meant walking away from her. My immediate visceral disgust at that idea told me which way I was leaning. No fucking way. I'd just tasted her. For the first time in six years, I could feel something. I wasn't giving that up now.

"So, how about I walk you to work?"

She lifted a brow. "I don't need you to walk me to work."

I crossed my arms and stared down at her. "Pardon me if I'm wrong, but weren't we mugged last night? And don't you have to still walk that same way to work? Wouldn't it be better if you walked with someone?"

She wrinkled her nose. "Why have I never noticed that when you speak sense, you're kind of annoying?"

I grinned. "So, what will it be?"

With an eye roll, she licked the rest of the sugar off her thumb. "Let me finish getting dressed."

"Excellent." I did love getting my way.

5

W hy was he being so protective and authoritative? I didn't usually like authoritative. It got my hackles up.

It's also incredibly sexy.

Sweet Marcus was easy to backburner. *Authoritative* Marcus had enough edge to him to make me pulse in places.

Also, when was the last time someone worried about you?

He waited dutifully for me to finish getting dressed and to put all my dishes away, all the while just chatting amiably. Poking around my apartment, but not really poking, just looking. As we walked downstairs and out of the building, he held the door, and then he did the oddest thing.

Well, it was odd to me. But he insisted on walking on the outside of the sidewalk when I tried to do it because I was worried about him. What if Stannis had seen him, gotten a picture, ran it through fucking visual recognition, and knew where to find him?

Stop it. Stannis knows nothing about him. Stannis is after you. He won't risk taking out a civilian in broad daylight.

Victus was a brutal organization, but the reason they were so hard to infiltrate and take down was because they were secretive. Discreet. If they wanted Marcus dead, they'd have killed him in his bed and made it look like an apparent heart attack. Or a hit and run at night... or a *mugging gone wrong*. The safest place Marcus could be was out in public. There was safety in having many eyes observing. I needed to relax. My team would deal with this.

Fucking Stannis Prochenko. This was the last thing I wanted to be dealing with. But of course, the Blood Stone mission was coming back to haunt me. I hadn't exactly dealt with Prochenko then, but I'd dealt with Victus. This had to be related. There was no such thing as coincidence.

Two years ago, we'd broken up a diamond smuggling ring. Victus had been in charge of it. They were using the proceeds to fund criminal activities. We'd gotten several members of Victus. But Prochencko had slipped our net. I had to wonder if he'd seen my face during that operation, and maybe that was why he'd come after me.

"Why are you so tense?" Marcus's whiskey-hoarse voice broke through my reverie.

I glanced up at him in surprise. How did he notice? I was usually able to project calm, amiable chatter. It was part of the cover.

He continued. "There's something about the set of your shoulders. You're tight, and you keep drumming your fingers against your thigh."

I frowned and looked down at my hands. "I used to play piano. When I'm nervous, I play Bologne in my head."

He blinked in surprise. "The composer? Why are you nervous?"

He said it with that velvet voice of his. While the British

accent had always been sexy, I'd never noticed just how deep his voice was. How sexy, enticing, almost like a constant invitation to lean in and lick something. "Um, I just... I don't know. Somehow it feels different. You know, when you almost get killed with someone."

He chuckled softly. "You mean when you're dating someone."

I laughed. "We are not dating. This is not what dating looks like."

He shrugged. "This is what dating looks like for me. Doing something nice, walking the woman I'm dating to work if I have the chance. I don't have to get started till ten or so."

I wanted to tell him I was capable of doing this by myself. But of course he knew that, and that would just be me acting ornery. He was being nice. I could do nice.

I wasn't kidding when I'd told him there was something more interesting about him now. I kept thinking about last night when he'd literally stepped in front of a gun with his body to protect me. The only people that did that for me were my partners. People I worked with. You trust each other in the field, like family. I'd never had anyone else do that for me.

You've had it. Your parents.

I swallowed that stinging burn of pain.

"Well, it's nice. And I appreciate it."

He casually threw an arm around my shoulder, and I glanced down at it, willing the electric lightning bolts in my body to calm their tits. It was just a casual arm across the shoulder. Totally casual. This was not a time for my libido to finally jump to attention.

Not to worry. We already jumped to attention last night.

God.

"You know, I feel like we need a re-do of all of our dates. I feel like we didn't really get to know each other."

I swallowed hard and watched him warily. "What do you mean?"

"Well, for starters, you're a badass. All your badassery came out to play, and I dug it. I mean, I'd prefer you didn't chase homicidal muggers, but still, total badass. It was hot."

I laughed. "What, because I am reckless and took off chasing after an armed psychopath, you want to date me?"

He shrugged. "Well, it showed you had spunk. I get the impression you hold yourself tightly together all the time. You hold a façade in place. But underneath is someone lively, maybe sometimes a little reckless. But it's someone who has spirit to live. It made me see you in a whole new way."

My steps faltered. He saw too much. All the things I *didn't* want him to see.

He needed to see the bland, boring, nice girl who watched too much reality TV, which I did, and perhaps drank too many Nationals on my couch with Addie. That was my idea of a wild night out. He was supposed to see *that* woman, not anything deeper.

His gaze searched mine. "You're sad now. I'm not trying to make you uncomfortable."

My nose stung from the sudden well of emotion. "No, you're not—" I shook my head. What the fuck was wrong with me? I was getting gushy just because someone saw me a little too clearly? "You're not making me uncomfortable. It's just that I remembered the story about how my parents met. Some guy was harassing my mom near where she lived. And my dad happened upon it and shooed him off then walked her to work. They used to talk about how they fell in love on that walk, you know?"

"That's a beautiful story."

"Yeah, it is. Just... You doing this reminds me of that."

"So that's a good memory, right?"

I nodded with a smile and then started walking again. "Yeah, it's a good memory. They passed away when I was eighteen, so it's bittersweet."

"Shit. I'm so sorry."

"No, you're fine. I guess I never told you that."

He shook his head. "No. But do you see what I mean? We're going to have to do our first and second date, at the very least, all over again."

I laughed. "You're not what I expected."

"Well, neither are you. Which I'm pretty sure is fantastic."

"You're more stubborn than I thought. Chivalrous, yes, but a little commanding. You like to be in charge. You are concerned about my safety. It's nice to be worried about."

He grinned. "Who doesn't like to be in charge?"

"I don't know, someone out there over the rainbow, I guess."

He chuckled. "Those aren't the words."

I shrugged. "I know that."

He lifted a brow. "Do you?"

At the light, he took my hand and we crossed the street. I expected him to let it go, but he didn't. A zing of electricity shot up my arm, making my body vibrate and my thighs clench together as something pulled deep and low in my belly. "So, we're holding hands now?"

"Yep. I decided I wanted to hold your hand on the second date, but then obviously we were interrupted."

I wrinkled my nose and laughed. "Oh God. Because of

your food poisoning. I'm so sorry. That sushi restaurant was supposed to be the best."

His brow furrowed. "Yeah, you know I'm not opposed to trying it again."

I laughed and shook my head. "No, no, no, no. Don't you get that thing where if something makes you sick you can never look at it again?"

He shook his head. "No. Because what if you're wrong about the thing that made you sick?"

"No, really, we don't have to."

He laughed. "Well, for you I'd be willing to risk it. And I do want to finish that bowling match. Although you were kicking my arse."

"I was, wasn't I?"

His laugh was deep and rich, and to me it felt like a sip of smoky brandy by the fire on a cold night. It was the most outstanding thing I'd ever heard in my life.

"I was letting you win."

"You were not," I squeaked out with a laugh.

God, this was dating? This was nice. Why had I been avoiding it?

You know why.

Yes, I did know why. Fucking Tyler Warden. To be fair, the disaster of that relationship was mostly my fault. I'd believed him and his lies. I should have known better. After all, wasn't that what all that training with Roz was for? So I'd be able to spot people like him? The pretenders?

But this was different. *Marcus Black* was different. Just a normal guy. A video game designer who liked holding my hand and wanted me to keep kicking his ass at bowling. I could do this.

And besides, he made me feel alive. *Really* alive, not that sort of adrenaline-numbed feeling like when I was on a mission. He made me want to laugh properly and do silly things. Was this that balance everyone kept speaking of?

Must be.

As we approached my building, I tried to extricate my hand, but he held on. "What, embarrassed to be seen with me?"

I started to laugh. "Oh God, it's not that. I can see the girls running out now to ogle you. You're very handsome, but I think you know that already."

He just gave me a lopsided grin, a flash of white teeth, his stubble making him look even sexier. It wasn't fair. "I'd like to meet your work friends, but maybe after we go on a couple dates first. In case they're crazy."

I laughed. "My best friend Addie, she *is* crazy. But no, I'm not embarrassed, I promise. It's just... We're *not* dating."

"*Yes*, we are. We're even holding hands, look." He held our intertwined hands up when I shook my head.

"God, you're so annoying—"

"Lyra?"

I whipped around, my hand still intertwined with Marcus's. And my stomach dropped. I dropped his hand immediately and swallowed hard. "Tyler. What, um... What are you doing here?"

His gaze flickered from me to Marcus, narrowed slightly, and then settled back onto my hand that had just been intertwined with Marcus's. "Well, I guess Roz didn't tell you. Given the shift with the new clients, I've been transferred here indefinitely."

At that dropped bomb, my stomach snapped back into place, but this time it tossed and splashed bile, which crawled up my throat begging to be expelled. I swallowed again, trying to keep it all down, push it down like my feelings about this whole fucked-up situation. Why would Roz not tell me?

"Oh. I wasn't aware. It's busy season, you know, with all the award shows coming up."

He grinned. "Yeah. You know I love nothing more than giving a starlet what she wants."

"Right, starlets, of course. Well, we won't keep you."

I thought Tyler would just go away so I could gather myself. Think, breathe, get my thoughts together for just a minute. I hadn't seen him in over a year. He normally worked out of London since he'd been transferred after our fake relationship. We hadn't even had an op together, which made sense because he was normally assigned as an undercover Valentine agent. His specialty was to get women to fall in love with him. That was his job. And then he got them to betray the men that they claimed to love.

But instead of opening the massive glass door and stepping inside, he turned to Marcus. "We haven't met. Are you new here?"

Marcus watched him with narrowed eyes and crossed his arms over his massive chest. "No. I was just walking Lyra to work."

Tyler's brows lifted. "Oh. Well, that's nice of you. Is that your job or something?"

Marcus didn't take the bait. Instead, he wrapped an arm around my waist, leaned down, and said, "I'll see you back at the flat."

I noticed what he did there. That one line made it sound like we lived together.

I opened my mouth to correct him but noticed Tyler had adopted that same crossed-arm look. "Oh, so you're what, together? Oh, Lyra, look at you, slumming it."

My eyes went wide. "Excuse me?"

Tyler gave him an equal smirk. "Oh, right. Sorry. We used to date."

Marcus just laughed smoothly. "Yeah, I gathered. Well, mate, wish I could say it was good to meet you, but I'd like to kiss my girlfriend now."

Girlfriend. He just called me his... Oh God. I turned to stare at him, and he was giving me a look. I knew what that *look* meant, and I just went with it. He leaned in and brushed his lips over mine, and God, he tasted like mint and sin and sex, and he was doing me a favor.

When I parted my lips, he deepened the kiss just enough to make me want more. One sweep of his tongue to make me a promise. To make me *ache*. And then he pulled back. "Have a great day at work, Lyra. I'll see you back at home, yeah?"

I was left just staring after him, my lips still tingling, my body thrumming. What just happened?

Tyler's gaze flickered over me. "Well, will wonders never cease? You're not the young ingenue anymore, are you? Now you look like a woman who actually knows what she's doing. I can't help feeling a little proud."

I glared at him. "You had nothing to do with it. Now if you'll excuse me, I have work to do."

I turned my back on him, not waiting for him to open the heavy glass doors for me. I marched with purpose through our lobby and punched my PIN code at the inner entrance to log in to the system. The doors opened and I was free. I knew that Tyler was going to have to type his own code in, so I only had seconds to escape. Instead of waiting for the elevator, I took the stairs as quickly as I could.

And tried to tell myself I wasn't running from him.

Lyra

My heart pounding, my nerves shot, I tried for steadying breaths as I headed straight for Roz's office. But she wasn't in there.

Most of the agents were at their stations in the main bank of desks and cubicles. There were several meetings going on in the corner briefing rooms, but my mentor was nowhere to be found. Where the hell was Roz?

I'd settle for Addie right now, but I knew she'd opt to poison Tyler on the spot, and I needed answers that did not include murder at the moment. After ten minutes of searching for Roz, I had no choice but to head to my station. I was located in a semi-private corner with Addie and another field agent, Mick. Mick was on a long-term assignment in Yemen, so for the past three months, it had just been Addie and I.

My gaze bounced around the room, looking for my ill-fated ex, but there was no sign of him... or Roz. I didn't have any other choice; I had to go about my job. I filled out reports from the mugging and continued working on a briefing about an Albanian smuggling crew until the briefing on Victus was scheduled to begin in thirty minutes.

Addie had zero chill when she found me at my desk. "Holy fuck, Lyra. Have you seen—"

I beat her to the punch. "Tyler? Yeah, I saw him as I was walking in. You know, with Marcus."

Addie's eyes lit up. "Marcus. As in your date, *Marcus*?"

"Yes. He thinks we're dating now."

Addie choked out a laugh. "What?"

"Yeah, I know. He thinks that last night I showed him a

side of myself I never have before. Which is, of course, *accurate*. But now, especially since I told him I don't think we *should* date, not that I didn't want to date, he thinks we *are* dating. And he insisted on walking me here today, where we ran into *Tyler*."

Her wide eyes bugged out in her expressive face. "Oh my God, how did that go? What did Tyler say?"

"Tyler was an asshole. He tried to posture, though for what reason I have no idea. It makes no sense. Especially after the way that ended."

Addie just laughed. "Oh my God, it makes so much sense. He didn't want you, but now that he sees someone else wants a toy from his toy box, he wants to pee all over it."

"I'm not a toy. And he can fuck right off."

Addie clapped. "Amen, sister. What are you going to do?"

I tugged on one of my curls as it tickled my ear. "I don't know what to do. This is not how any of this is supposed to happen. I was *never* supposed to see him again. After all, what reason would I have to see him again? He wasn't even stationed here, but now he's been transferred."

Addie winced. "Yeah, a Victus sighting, that's kind of a big deal. As soon as you called in last night, Roz made some calls. I guess he was on the first plane."

I slouched into my seat, trying to melt into my turquoise chair. "Fuck. I can't stare at him all day every day."

"Well, the difference is now you're not pining after him."

I frowned at her. "I was never pining."

"Well, more along the lines of he lied to you and you believed him. And yes, that makes him a dick, but you don't believe him anymore. And it turns out you have someone even hotter on the radar."

"You don't even know if he's hotter."

She smiled sheepishly. "I'll have you know I had a look at your dating profile and saw who you were going out with. You know, just to double-check and make sure you were going to be okay. I ran my own background check on Marcus Black, and you're right. He is a standup guy. One of his games is hugely popular."

"Really?" I blinked in surprise.

She nodded. "You weren't curious? Let me guess, you just looked at the facts. Family, friends, job. No fine details."

"Uh, I'm not really one for video games, and I wanted to get those finer details, you know... from dating him."

She rolled her eyes. "Sometimes you are such a traditionalist. I played his game. It's good times. I played with Luke downstairs."

I wrinkled my nose. Luke was a wet works specialist. Basically one of the assassins. All of us agents thought we were better than they were. We weren't, but we liked to believe we were. The assassins were called in mostly for cleanup jobs. At least we did intelligence as well. "Ahh, Luke."

She waved me off. "He's just a bit of fun when I'm bored. But anyway, about your Marcus. I mean look, he is a hottie first of all. And he's smart. And apparently he has a protective streak too."

I smiled. "I know, right?" And despite my automatic reflex to keep myself hidden, I liked him.

"Yes. And from what I can tell, he's unlikely to murder you when you're sleeping. I looked into him as far back as elementary school because you know how sometimes you can tell that someone's going to be a serial killer based on how they used to act in the schoolyard. He did once punch a boy called Jason Sims because he used a very bad word to a girl, but I only found that because it was written up."

"You looked into his primary school in England?"

She nodded and smiled. "Yes, in this little village called Knotsworth. But he had a nice little family and everything."

I sighed. "Addie, thank you. But you didn't need to do that. I already looked him up."

"Did you look at his primary school though?"

I laughed. "No, but I thank you for being extra thorough."

"You're welcome. What are besties for? Besides, it looks good for you to be dating. You know full well they won't promote you to senior agent unless you look more settled. Do what you need to do."

I winced. "Well, you don't have to tell me twice. I know what I *need* to do. I just want to do it on my own timeline. Did I tell you he sort of indicated to Tyler that we were an item?"

She blinked at me. "He what?"

"Tyler was being a dick, and Marcus wrapped his arm around me and said he'd see me back at the flat, making it seem like we lived together."

Addie's eyes went big. "Oh my God, I'm in love with him. I'm going to have his babies. True story. Let's be a throuple."

I laughed. "And then he kissed me. Like not just a chaste, *okay see you later, love* kind of thing. More like in a *hey, I'll see you later and I plan to shag you against the wall* kind of way."

"Oh boy, first of all I love that he's British and you're already saying his Briticisms. Second of all, if he does *shag* you against the wall, can you please call me and tell me all about it? And finally, I would have killed to see the look on Tyler's face. *Killed.*"

My timer went off, and I knew it was time for the Victus briefing. "Ugh, we should head down. I wanted to talk to Roz before the briefing, but I guess she's busy."

"She is. She was in there talking to Browning. He was

shouting, as he's prone to do, about security measures, how the hell someone found one of his agents, how the hell Victus was being allowed to run around in our backyard, and what we need to do about it."

I frowned. "Wow, okay. So I guess everybody knows."

"Oh hon, don't worry about it. This isn't on you."

"Yeah, but I'm the one who let him get away."

She knew better than to argue with me since I *had* let him get away because I'd been worried about the civilian that I was with.

"Stop worrying. They're taking it seriously. Roz might not want you to be the one on this."

Like hell would I sit this one out. "Oh, I'm on this. Whether she wants me or not."

Addie sighed. She knew me.

When we reached the briefing room, Browning was already there. He marched right up to me. "You're well, Agent Wilkinson?" William Browning was the section head of our branch of The Firm.

I nodded. "Yes, sir. I'm fine. I just wish I'd been able to bring him in last night."

He shook his head. "You were with a civilian, yes?"

I nodded. "Yes, sir. It was either let Prochenko go or blow my cover."

"You made the right decision. Roz and I were just talking about it. Come in. Take a seat. We'll brief the rest of the team."

I frowned at Browning's back as he marched to the head of the table. He was being nice. He was *never* nice. Ever. I didn't even think the man knew how to be nice.

There was something weird about this. Were they worried I'd been compromised?

When Roz started the meeting, she brought everyone on

the team up to speed on Victus. And I surreptitiously turned around to see who was in the briefing room.

Everyone.

Jesus Christ. It was practically standing room only. So everybody was going to know that I had fucked up.

Next time don't fuck up.

Usually I liked to have my massive fuck ups in private. Take responsibility and deal with them appropriately. But now, everyone was hearing all about my mistakes last night.

A familiar voice from somewhere near the back piped up. "Just what was Agent Wilkinson doing last night when she encountered Prochenko?"

I ground my teeth. Fucking Tyler. What in the world? Why had I ever, ever, ever thought that I cared about him?

It was Browning who answered, not Roz.

"She was off duty. Which is even more concerning. How is it that Victus knows the movement of our agents?" He clicked the button to show the next slide. "Senior management has been reviewing Agent Wilkinson's movements over the last six weeks. Nothing untoward has occurred. She's been following movement protocols. So this isn't a breach. This was either luck or something larger."

I hated that I was under constant surveillance. Only senior agents lost the big brother eye.

Roz stood up then. "Our intel indicates something larger. Victus is in the market for a weapon."

I spoke up then. "What kind of weapon?"

"Something so new it's not even on the market yet. The Annihilator. In essence, it sends some kind of radiation pulse that causes a rapid acceleration of charged particles. So it's not a bullet. It's a wave of radiation."

She pressed a button on the remote control she was holding, and a video began, showing us what a weapon like that could do to a human body.

I winced. It showed a man being shot at, with protective gear on, and his body flying backward.

When the camera panned in, his skin looked charred and burned.

But there were no points of entry on him. No bullet wounds, no explosion. I whistled low. "There's a weapon like that?"

She nodded. "It's highly experimental. It was built by this man,"—she clicked a button to stop the video, and a slide appeared on the screen—"Dr. Ryan Dodd, a military contractor. Dr. Dodd went missing about six weeks ago. From what we can gather, he either went to ground or someone took him. Victus is in town to meet with a weapons broker who may either have Dodd, know where to find him, or have gotten their hands on the weapon. We will send out a team to pick up the broker and bring him in so we can question him."

Before my hand even went up, Browning announced, "It will be a three-person team. Agents Tyler Warden, Lyra Wilkinson, and Adaline Franklin."

My mouth hung open. Why Addie? And my God, why the fuck Tyler?

When we were dismissed, Addie frowned. "I don't know why they would pick me."

We approached Roz, who waved us off. "I don't know why you were picked. You were Browning's choices. And as for Tyler, he has a lot of experience with Victus."

"Yes, I remember," I muttered. "But you couldn't have given me a heads-up that he was being transferred to our section?"

Her gaze narrowed on me. "Now is not the time for personal feelings, Lyra."

I ground my teeth as I fought to remain calm. "I hear you, but a little warning would have been nice."

"One of my agents was exposed to Victus. I was trying to cover your ass, so when was I supposed to warn you that your feelings were going to be at risk?"

I frowned. Roz wasn't usually so harsh with me. "I'm sorry."

"Well you know now," she muttered before marching off.

Addie frowned at me. "What's wrong with her?"

I shook my head. "I have no fucking idea."

"All right. Well, let's get ready. This recon is going to be a joy. My bestie and the man we both hate. Can't think of a better way to spend a Saturday."

I rolled my eyes. "Let's just get this over with. The sooner we get this done with, the sooner maybe Tyler will go back to that hole he crawled out of."

"Amen to that."

6

MARCUS

G oing into the office of Exodus was a rarity.

But this was important. I wanted to make certain Lyra was safe.

Rhodes followed behind me at a fast clip as we approached the darkened underground service elevator that led us into the interior of the building.

All parking was four levels down. The main floor was still subterranean. What was above looked like a condemned warehouse surrounded by barbed wire, a chemical spill sign, and the most state-of-the-art security system money could buy. That should be completely uninteresting to anyone.

In the elevator, Rhodes was quiet, but I could feel his surreptitious glances toward me. When the elevator finally opened, we stepped into the usual bustle of activity. Agents moving about. Briefings to attend, people to interrogate.

Everyone thought when you became a spy it was going to be glitz and glamor. I'd wondered about that. What it was going to be like, but the idea was to make this place as uninteresting as possible. There was a reason we only came here for briefings.

The hallways were lit with fluorescents. The walls were a muted gray. Not much art, and what was there was heavy and dark. You could clearly tell a man had chosen all the decorations.

I gave a nod to Felix in the armory and then marched down to threat assessment. Threat assessment was open on all sides with glass walls. But it was sunken in, so you had to step down. The floors were lit though, giving it a brighter and techier feel. It was in there that we learned about the world's nastiest creatures that needed putting down.

Our command for Exodus at this station, whom we knew only as Michael, glowered up at me when I jogged down the stairs. "Ah, Marcus. Always causing trouble."

"Sir."

He gave me a brief nod. "So today I get a sir. I like that change."

I refrained from rolling my eyes. "What do we have?"

He tapped a couple of buttons as Rhodes and Maggie, one of the senior officers, joined us. Her heels made a *clip-clop* sound as she took the stairs down, and she gave me a warm smile. "Marcus. It's nice to see you."

"Maggie, ma'am."

She waved her hand. "I'm not like this idiot who likes the sir title. Maggie's fine. You know that."

I shrugged, nonetheless. Considering Maggie had tried to shove her hand down my pants on a mission two years ago, I liked to keep some formality between us. She was also responsible for my psychological assessment, so even more distance was required. Though considering I had turned her down, she never held it against me. It was like she really could compartmentalize.

I had yet to meet another single agent who properly could.

She asked, "Where are we on Victus?"

Michael tapped a few buttons, and on the screen appeared the man I had been chasing. "That's him," I said.

Michael nodded. "Yes. Stannis Prochenko. Low-level member of Victus. He's not important enough for us to have flagged him, but the fact that he's here led us into a deep dive."

Maggie stepped forward, sliding tablets over to Rhodes and myself. "Victus is after this weapon. They call it the Annihilator. Stannis is here to make a deal either for the creator himself or the actual weapon. We're not sure which. And we don't know where Stannis is at this moment. But we do know who he's meeting and where."

Michael pulled up a photo of a tall, pale white man with white-blond hair and harsh hawkish features.

"Who is that?" I asked.

"His name is Mads McLean," Michael said. "His mother is Dutch, his father Irish and former IRA. Mads doesn't have any of those affiliations. He's a freelancer. Classic story, always in trouble as a youth, in and out of jail. His psychological profile indicates he's your garden variety psychopath. He is a middleman brokering a weapons deal. He's going to meet with Stannis to have Victus enter their bid. It's a very unique bidding strategy. As a middleman, he travels from buyer to buyer, gets them to enter their code, and their cash is held in escrow. If they win the bid, all funds are paid to the seller, and the losing bidders' funds are returned. I suppose they think that none of the buyers are going to try and take out the others this way since all bids are private and there are only rumors as to who is entering the bidding process. What we want to do is catch hold of Mads here."

Maggie added, "To do that we need to follow Stannis. And intel says they will be meeting at the Venice in the City Bacchanal."

I furrowed my brow. "Isn't that just a glitzy rich people version of a fair?" I remembered photographs from the event last year. A who's who of Hollywood had been there. The whole event was ages eighteen and up, and things were purported to get wild. Sex and drugs. Each year they had an artist in residence and the fair was themed around them. "Who is the artist in residence?"

Maggie gave me a sardonic once-over. "Look at you with the culture."

She hesitated.

I knew when she was holding something back. "Who is it Maggie?

"It's Nicola Wessex."

The moment she said the name, I could picture the brunette with the big smile and slightly too small eyes. She specialized in sculpture, but also liked performance art. "Brunette artist. Sculptor, right?"

"I keep forgetting that you literally remember every-thing." With a click of the remote she changed the screen. "Her record is clean. She's actually an artist. But she showed up on some mission briefs as a sibling to a Fredrick Kozol.

My eyebrows snapped down. "Her brother is Victus?"

Maggie nodded. "Half-brother, but yes. She grew up with her mother in Tahoe and had very little interaction with her father when she was little and none since she became an adult. As far as our intel shows, she met her brother Fredrick once when they were both adults, but they haven't had any real interactions or connections since then. Still though, Fredrick has taken an interest in her art. She has a foundation that funds arts programs for children around the world, and Fredrick has contributed quite a bit of money to it. Granted we can only see that from the bank transfers because he's publicly quiet, leaving her to do her thing. It's possible she doesn't even know the depths of what he's capable of."

I worked my jaw as I read through her profile. All roads led to fucking Victus.

"Okay, what time's the meet?" Rhodes asked.

"We don't know. We have trackers on Stannis now. When he's on the move, you will get a notification."

I looked at Michael. "All right, so basically be at the event, intercept and bring in Mads."

Michael nodded. "Yes. You are on verification and identification. Rhodes is your second and in charge of pick up, and we'll give you a sniper as a third, just in case."

I nodded. "Who's the sniper?"

Maggie shrugged. "Becker's available. So is Carson. Both are excellent."

I preferred Becker, hands down. She was efficient, and most important, on missions she was deadly silent. You never heard from her unless you needed to. Carson talked too fucking much. He'd annoy me to death.

We all understood how I preferred to work, so everyone muttered, "Yeah, Becker."

Maggie nodded. "One small detail."

I rubbed at the back of my neck, eager to get back to the flat. "What's the problem?"

"The party is invitation only. And it's being pushed as a couples-only event. So Becker and Rhodes we can get in with staff. But you will need to walk in the front door. You'll have the greatest freedom of movement. But you'll need to be in a couple. They are very strict on this as part of the invitation. So I'll need to pair you with an agent."

I didn't like the flicker of interest in her gaze. "I'll take care of it."

She lifted a delicately arched brow. "Are you sure? I could—"

I cut her off before she could get too far down that train of thought. "This mission is classified top secret, yes?"

Michael nodded. "Yes. You couldn't divulge the real reason we're there."

"Okay then, better not take one of ours. I'll bring a civilian. Just get us an invite."

Are you insane? You don't want Lyra near this.

I didn't. And I was sure I was insane. But I wasn't letting Maggie paw me in public. No way no how.

"Great, tablets will be updated. You will be on standby for the next several days."

I nodded and turned to leave, but Michael called me back. "Actually, Marcus, we're not done."

Rhodes gave me a tap on the shoulder, and Maggie smiled as she excused herself as I turned to face the man who had been my mentor. "Yes, sir?"

He studied me with shrewd eyes. "Well, how did it go?"

I shrugged. "What do you mean?"

"No need to be so cagey. Curtis already let me know you were on a date."

"Sir, I prefer not to gossip. We have mission parameters."

Michael laughed. "God, am I that uptight?"

I shrugged. "Sir?"

"I trained you. Therefore, you must be a reflection on me.

And because you are stiff as a board, it makes me wonder if that's how I present myself."

"It's just that there's nothing to say, sir. I was out with a civilian. I know mission parameters. Secrecy always and preserve civilian life. I couldn't have gone after Prochenko without putting her in danger."

He sighed. "No, what I mean is, did you actually like her? Command, as you know, has been eyeing you for senior agent status. Command obviously doesn't like that you are a bit of a maverick, a free agent."

"Understood, sir. At the same time, I'm not going to do something just because it looks good to Command."

His lips quirked in a semblance of a lopsided smile. "And I would expect nothing less. I'm just interested, because as my pick for our next senior agent, you're an excellent candidate. And if you are making strides that make you look better, I'm interested and enthusiastic about it."

I gave him a sharp nod. I didn't like considering dating Lyra, or anyone else for that matter, as a way to make me look like a better candidate. I liked her. She'd kneed a terrorist in the nuts and lived to tell the tale. She had spunk. She was brilliant. And yeah, she was well fit. The way her gorgeous dark brown skin always seemed to glow, and her hair changed practically on a daily basis, but I liked it best when it was natural, fresh out of the shower, springy sweet curls always bouncing around her face. Always tempting me to reach out and touch a curl. Which obviously, I knew better. Dating Lyra Wilkinson would make me look good to Command, yes. But I didn't want her because she made me look good; I just wanted her. And she was going to need some convincing. So I needed Command to stay the fuck out of my love life because I didn't need the extra pressure.

"Sir, she's a civilian. I'm not sure where it's going. Right now, my only concern is keeping her safe."

He sighed. "I know you don't like us in your personal life, but that's part of the deal. You understood that when you signed on the dotted line."

"Yes, I did. Right now, she's my concern. Victus is a problem. If you want to talk about this after we catch them, I'd be open to that."

He gave me a nod that said I was dismissed, and I turned on my heel to go. I needed to keep her off their radar. No matter what.

Lyra

"Oh, this isn't awkward at all," I said and shifted in the passenger seat as I slid Tyler a glance.

"I see you looking at me." His voice was silk. But I knew better than to trust it.

"Mainly because I can't believe what I'm seeing." *Pompous prick.*

"You want to go ahead and ask all your questions, find out what I've been doing and get it out of your system?" he asked with a cheeky grin.

I opened my mouth to tell him what a pompous prick he was being but then shut it when Addie beat me to it on the comms. "You are such a pompous prick. Do you really think she's been worried about you or what you've been doing?"

Tyler chuckled low under his breath as he glanced around, checking his binoculars. "The way she's looking at me suggests that she's missed me. We all know how well that turned out last time."

My hands were balled up into little fists, and I was grateful that Addie couldn't see me. She was positioned in a tower overlooking our location. We were in the car, across the street from where Stannis's contact was supposed to be hiding out.

"I know you like to tell yourself she was hung up on you, but she wasn't. That was just your fragile ego talking."

Goddamn, I loved Addie. Even though I *had* been distraught, but only because I hadn't known the rules of the game. I hadn't known I was a job to him. Break in the new agent. But I wasn't dumb enough to make that mistake again.

He had broken me in all right. Singled me out, made me feel special, appreciated, seen, loved. Then, just when I was feeling a breath of confidence and fully coming into myself, he yanked the rug out from under me. Apparently, Roz thought I was getting too attached. And she was right. I was too attached. I'd started to need him.

The following three months had been the worst. Working through heartache and betrayal. He told me everything when he broke up with me though. Right down to how Roz had worked my profile. What I needed, how he was to treat me. It had all been completely orchestrated. I felt betrayed. Broken. And he'd come out unscathed, while I'd been shellshocked.

Over the years, I'd come to realize that Roz was, in her own intense way, trying to keep me out of the clutches of somebody who could've done real damage. If I had fallen for someone on the outside, someone who could've really broken my heart, I'd have been done for at The Firm. And it would have shattered everything I'd been working toward. So it had been better that it was with Tyler. And he *had* been gentle. I *had* felt loved and cherished. *Except none of it was real, was it?*

I swallowed and shook my head. "We're not doing this."

"If you say so. Are you really dating that Neanderthal?"

My head whipped around. "Just focus on the mission. My dating life is none of your concern."

"Just saying, he made it my concern by putting on that public display in front of me. Does he know about us?"

"There's no 'us' to know about, Tyler. As you relished in telling me many times, we weren't real. There was nothing to tell."

"Ah, right, so he doesn't know that I was your first. That you were in love."

"He doesn't need to know because you're inconsequential." I kept my emotions under tight control.

Over the mic, Addie laughed. "Oh, burn."

As much as I loved her, I wished she wasn't listening. I wished she wasn't present for my humiliation.

But that was unavoidable.

Tyler's voice went softer then. "I know you were hurt. That wasn't my intention. I was just doing my job."

The fury burned under my skin, making its way to the surface like steam, waves of heat on asphalt. "When I say we're not doing this, we're not doing this. Don't act like you didn't have a part in it. At any moment, you could've told me the truth."

"You were a mission. An op. That's all."

"Right. And at some point, you could've been less convincing. But you weren't."

He sighed. "That was the job. I don't know what to tell you. That's what it was. I never intended to hurt you. Once I realized you didn't know any of the rules, I tried to be as gentle as I could be. I didn't want you to be hurt."

I rolled my eyes and chuckled. "Right. We've been through this. We're not rehashing it again."

"I did care—"

At the corner of one of the buildings we were watching, I saw someone hopping down onto a stack of milk crates on the side of the building. I grabbed my binoculars. "We have a runner. Tall, pale, white-blond hair. He's making a beeline. Addie, do you see him?" Why was he running? You only ran if you were scared. And you were only scared for one reason.

Like someone told you to be scared.

He'd been warned. But by who?

"He's headed west."

"Copy. On my way." Then I shouted to Tyler. "Get me a fucking ID on him."

"Already sent the image in. Move your ass." The binoculars were already plugged into our tech. All imagery captured was already being sent to The Firm. We'd have something in mere moments.

I jumped out of the car, and Tyler followed. I could hear his heavy footfalls behind mine. I was lighter and a better long-distance runner, but he was stronger and faster, and he caught me easily as we chased the guy down. In our earpieces, Addie muttered, "He's going north now."

When we came up the side of one of the warehouses, Tyler indicated he was going left.

So I went right. Weapon out, I was ready. Adrenaline poured through my veins in a steady, drumming flutter, heightening all my senses to the bitter acrid odor in the air. It smelled like dust and turpentine. I shifted on my feet, trying to stay calm and read the shift of the air around me.

There was a rustling noise on my left, and I immediately went that way, listening for the answering footfall. That was when I felt the whoosh of air to my right. I ducked easily, and came up with an uppercut, hitting the man right under his jaw. His head snapped back, and I tapped my mic. "I have him, north entrance."

When I lunged for him, he jammed his elbow back, catching me on my cheekbone. I staggered back, wincing at the pain.

He swung again, and I blocked him and kneed him in the nuts. But the son of a bitch adjusted his leg to provide some cover for his nuts because he stayed upright.

He gave me a nasty grin and landed a kick straight in my midsection. I tightened my core, but it wasn't enough, and all the air whooshed out of me as I went flying three feet backward.

I landed in a pile of boxes, and he took off.

Addie's voice rang in my comms as she said, "He's running. Headed east."

Tyler's voice followed hers. "I have an ID. Mads McLean. Weapons broker. Likely Stannis's contact." Why the fuck didn't Tyler even sound winded?

You're okay. Get the hell up.

But Christ, a kick to the sternum really knocked out your air. When I rolled over and jumped back on my feet, I started running again. Hobbling was more like it.

Mads threw things in my path, but Tyler came running in from the other direction, and behind me, I could hear Addie approaching from the left as well.

Mads was caught. There was no way out.

But suddenly he whirled around and came running right at me, forcing my steps to falter so I wouldn't run right into him.

"You have nowhere to go. Give up. Work with us and we'll go easy—"

He barreled for me, grabbing me and taking me down. As

we rolled, he tried to aim punches, which I blocked. One of them landed though, right above the cheek where he'd gotten me before with the elbow. Right outside the socket of my eye. And I knew, *I knew* that was going to be a black eye.

I blocked one hand, landing a punch of my own and snapping his head back again. But then he came back with a massive open-palmed clap over my ears and set them ringing. A wave of nausea hit me hard, and the world spun. The dingy warehouse concrete was so cold it felt like ice beneath my body. And someone was tilting it, shaking it about. My head lolled from side to side. I could only watch in horror as Mads pulled a gun, aimed at one of my team members, and fired.

Tyler and Addie dove for cover. I could hear Addie yelling, "Fuck. Is she shot Tyler?"

Tyler's voice was uneven. Why did he sound like that? "I can't see her."

And then Mads McLean's weight was gone, and suddenly I could breathe. Sort of. God, when I tried to lift my head, that loud clanging sound rolled through me again.

I heard more gunfire, but not as close this time. And then all I heard were Tyler's shouted commands. "You stay there, I'm going after him."

Several seconds later, there were fingers palpating all over my body. I winced as they came near my sternum and then my face.

Addie said, "I want to do a quick check to make sure he didn't hit anything vitally important internally. You're going to be okay. You're going to have a nasty bruise though."

"Fuck, please God, tell me he didn't get away."

But Tyler's singular footsteps coming back told me what I already knew. Mads was gone. I leaned my head back on the cool concrete. "Fuck."

Tyler knelt down next to me. "She okay?"

Addie's voice was tense. "We're going to have to get her checked out when we're back. But yeah, I think she's fine."

His voice was soft as he spoke to me. "I'm sorry, Lyra. I didn't catch him. But he did drop this."

Why did his voice sound gentle? That wasn't what I needed. I needed this mission wrapped up so my life could return back to some normalcy. Because with Stannis Prochenko and his cronies gone, Tyler would be gone. And then my life would be my own again.

"What did he drop?"

He held up a heavy metallic card of some sort. On the back was a time scrawled in gold metallic ink and the initials, S. P.

I pushed to my feet and took the charcoal-colored metal card from him. It was a calling card for the Venice in the City Bacchanal. "We need an invite to this." The Bacchanal was one of the most exclusive parties in all of Los Angeles. Mads was our ticket to that weapon and our ticket to Stannis. If they were going to be there, so were we. We could get a two for one.

7

MARCUS

I was watching as Lyra climbed out of a cab. She was moving gingerly. As if she'd been hurt. I focused the camera lens on her face, and that's when I saw it... the bruising along the left side of her cheek. Like she'd been hit. Son of a bloody bitch. I put my binoculars away and marched to my door. I yanked it open just as she climbed the stairs to the landing. "Hey."

She startled and blinked rapidly. "Oh, Marcus. Hi."

I frowned at her, then indicated her eye. "What happened?"

"It's nothing. I was taking a kickboxing class with my best friend, Addie. Some idiot was overzealous. I got clipped."

She was lying. Okay, not *exactly* lying, but she was leaving something out. She'd told me just enough of the truth to make it believable, but what was she hiding? She obviously had other aches and pains and was moving gingerly, so why lie to me?

Nothing in her files indicated a history of abuse. so maybe she was telling the truth? But there was something about the way she hesitated with her smile that said she was holding something back from me.

Was it the bloke from earlier? She clearly hadn't been happy to see him. But they worked together, and when would he have had an opportunity to hurt her? Unless he was the one with the boxing gloves.

I was going to have to find out more about him.

Just like a stalker.

Had he hurt her before? There had been no police reports, but maybe she'd never reported anything.

The app had only matched us a month ago, and her file didn't mention anything about who she'd been with before that, but my instincts screamed this had something to do with the bloke at work.

One way or another I'd find out. And then I was going to hurt whoever had put his hands on her.

"Are you up for some food?" I asked her casually, knowing full well she was going to try and weasel out of it.

"You sure are persistent." She made her way to the top of the stairs, wincing lightly as she did. "All I need right now is a hot bath. No more kickboxing for me."

I should let it go. She was clearly wiped out. But if she wasn't going to tell me what the hell happened to her, I was going to figure it out myself. But at least I could feed her first.

"Yes, you clearly look like you need a hot bath, but you also need some food, and I can tell you don't feel like cooking it yourself. Besides, it'll give us a chance to continue our conversation from this morning."

Seeing her like that stirred a protective instinct I'd thought to be long dead. That thing I just reserved for my family, my brother, my mates... I felt it toward her.

Let's not get carried away with ourselves. You have only known her for a month.

I couldn't help it though.

"Thank you, but honestly, all I want to do is sleep." Her stomach betrayed her and growled so loudly it echoed down the hallway.

"Oh, so you're not hungry at all?"

"That's not fair. You can't use my grumbling stomach against me."

I shrugged. "Everything is fair. Go have a bath. I'll bring you something to eat."

"I don't want you going to any trouble. I think I have some yogurt and some frozen meals."

"Don't be ridiculous. You need real food. And it just so happens I cooked. So you go get in the bath. I'll be right over."

"You're very annoying." A deep furrow had formed between her brows. "Why can't you just ignore me?"

"First of all, if you think I can ignore you after we kissed, you undersell yourself. Secondly, if you think I can ignore you when you look so beat up and haggard, you underestimate my chivalry."

"Isn't chivalry dead?"

"Probably, yeah, if you're dealing with a Neanderthal. Go, get in the tub. I'll bring you something to eat."

Back in my flat, I carved out a portion of my mother's lasagna recipe, putting it in a container and placing the rest of it in the freezer. I also grabbed the bottle of red I had in the wine fridge.

I didn't know much about vintage wines. But Rhodes, for all his bluster and cockiness, the bastard knew wines. He would always go on and on about which one was the best and which ones to try. It had sort of rubbed off on me, so I always made it a point to keep my wine fridge full, hoping that I would somehow become someone totally different and finally learn to give a fuck about great wines. But no. I still didn't give a fuck. I still preferred a pint.

But Lyra looked like she could use a glass or two.

As I traipsed across the hall to Lyra's flat, I found Mrs. Washington in the hallway, and she gave me a broad grin. "It's so nice to see you and Lyra getting along so well."

I grinned at her. "Just being neighborly, Mrs. Washington." The saucy old broad knew exactly what I was up to.

She sniffed the air. "That's lasagna, young man. You bring my mail up for me, bring me my heavy packages, but never, not even once, have you brought me lasagna."

I chuckled softly. "Mrs. Washington, if I thought you could stomach my cooking, I'd bake you some."

Her gaze travelled over me appreciatively, and I bit back a chuckle. "Oh, I'm willing to try, young man."

I made a mental note of that and gave her a wave as she stepped into her flat.

I knocked on Lyra's door, and it took her a moment to answer. When she did, she was in sweatpants. Her curls were wrapped up in a scarf, her face devoid of makeup, and I clenched my jaw at the up-close view of her bruise.

Jesus. From the looks of it, she was sore all over as well.

I kept my mouth shut though, and instead held up the container and the wine. "You have to eat. I know you're famished."

She blinked in surprise. "What in the world?" Her nose twitched as the scent of the garlic hit her. "Is this homemade?"

"Yes. And don't tell me you don't need it and you're just going to get a doughnut because that's bullshit. I had more than enough. So when you're done with the container, just bring it back, okay?"

"You made lasagna?" She practically tore the container out of my hands.

"Yes. Matter of fact I did."

"You can cook?"

I laughed and ran my hand through my hair. "Yes. I regularly get hungry, so it was bound to happen."

"Oh my God, you're killing me, you know that?"

I was pleased by how surprised she seemed. "And just how am I doing that? By bringing you food? Trust me, it's not poisonous. And from the sound of it, you're hungry."

She stared at the wine. "And you brought me wine too."

I held up the bottle of wine and grinned. "You looked like you'd had a hell of a day. Under normal circumstances, I'd suggest we eat together. But you look wiped."

She sagged in relief. "So you noticed."

"I did."

Lyra leaned against her door frame as she gnawed on a piece of garlic bread. "Jesus, why are you tempting me?"

I grinned at that and then shoved my hands in my pockets. "You seem like you want to be tempted."

She shook her head. "I was serious when I said I did not have time for a relationship."

"Well, aren't you presumptuous? Who said I want a relationship? I was willing to let you use me for my body."

She coughed a laugh, and there was almost a hysterical hint to it. "Jesus, Marcus, why now? Why are you this *now*? Why weren't you *this* earlier?"

"I don't know what—" When she lifted her gaze to mine, I saw there were tears shining in her eyes, and I couldn't help myself. I closed the gap between us and pulled her in and wrapped my arms around her. "Hey, you're okay. You're fine."

No. This was not fine. This was dangerous.

You want to take care of her. If you brought danger to her doorstep, you might need to leave. Don't get too close.

But still, I couldn't get my arms to unlock. "Hey, you're okay. Seems like you've had a long couple of days."

"You don't know the half of it." She sighed into my chest where she'd buried her head.

"Look, I know you're not sure if we're a thing, but if you want to talk, I'm here."

She blinked up at me, the tears brimming. "You're too nice."

I flashed a grin then. "Most people wouldn't say that about me."

"Well, most people are idiots."

"Maybe."

"They mostly aren't paying attention anyway. Marcus, I really wish to God that I could do this. I *want* to do this. But I can't."

"Hey, relax. *This* isn't anything. This is just me bringing a neighbor dinner because she looked like she needed it."

She shifted her head up to mine, and then her gaze slipped to my lips. The tightening happened in my gut first and then hit my dick. The longer she stared, the longer every system in my body started to shut down all functions, making sure the blood flow was focused where it wanted to go.

Fuck, I wanted her.

I wanted her lips underneath mine. I wanted her making that sweet little moaning sound. Instead, I stopped. I forced my attention to her forehead, not her mouth. Not on those giant doe eyes, begging me to do the thing that I shouldn't.

Because I shouldn't want to do this. I shouldn't even be there. I should be looking for all avenues away from this. And despite the twitching protestations of my dick, I leaned forward and pressed a kiss to her forehead then stepped back. "Well, enjoy your night. I'll see you around, Lyra."

She blinked at me rapidly, and then frowned. "Oh, okay. Um, thank you?"

Her eyes were glazed, and her lips slightly parted. One flickering gaze at her chest told me that her nipples were erect and her breathing was shallow. She wanted me.

Yeah, well, join the party.

But it wasn't safe for her. And until I could make it safe, I probably needed to keep my distance.

So I turned around and forced myself to walk back down the hallway and let myself into my flat, locking the door behind me.

MARCUS

Lyra Wilkinson smelled like sunshine and coconuts.

I couldn't ignore the mental picture of her smile, her eyes. And her fucking scent... I could swear I smelled it every-where. Even when I was sleeping, my brain insisted on dreaming of her. Thinking about her. That little moan she made when I kissed her.

Bloody hell. I was toast.

When I went to bed, my brain had one dream locked down. Lyra in my arms on the night of our date, my lips on hers, her moaning. But this time, instead of that interruption by Stannis Prochenko, I kept kissing her. Kept stroking my tongue over hers until her knees were weak and she was gasping in my arms. Her arms looped around me, and that kiss became so much more than just a kiss. It became a promise. All from that moan.

In my delusional dream, I'd meant to be a perfect gentleman and deposit her at her door, but she let me in, and that kiss turned into so much more. My lips at her jaw, along her neck, and then lower. The tops of her breasts spilling out of her dress. Me brushing my stubble against her tender flesh, making her gasp.

Fucking hell. That moaning sound she made was becoming a constant hum, a constant promise. I couldn't let her go. But the tighter I tried to hold on, the more she became ethereal smoke, vanishing through my fingers.

I woke with sweat on my skin as the memory of the coconut lime scent of Lyra stayed with me. I flopped back onto my pillow. I really needed to get my shit together.

Put her out of your mind. There are larger issues at stake.

Easier said than done.

The buzzing that I had attributed to Lyra's moaning was actually my phone. There were texts after texts from Curtis. I rolled over and looked at the clock. It was four o'clock, 2:00 a.m. for him. I finally just picked up the phone and called him. "What's going on?"

"You're up. Good."

"I wasn't, but since you were texting me nonstop, now I am. What's going on?"

"Mads McLean was spotted in East LA today."

I sat up in bed. "When?"

"This afternoon. He was bleeding. Looks like he might have run into some trouble. He saw a known underground concierge doctor, one of ours. He planted a tracker on McLean. I've already patched everything through to your tablet. The meet between Mads and Prochenko is Saturday night at 10:00 p.m. at the Bacchanal. Think you'll be ready?"

"Do I get to question McLean first, or is it kill on sight?"

Curtis answered quickly. "We want him alive. We want to know who the new players are."

I could admit to myself that I was a little disappointed. "What about Prochenko? He came after me, Curtis."

"I know. And once we have the information we need, we'll figure out what we're going to do with him. But until then, bring him in breathing *and* talking too. Do you hear me?"

I sighed and glared at the clock. I wouldn't be sleeping now. Between my dream of Lyra and the situation with Prochenko, I might as well wake up. I sighed. "Yup, I'm on it."

"I'm serious, Marcus. We're not messing around, okay?"

"Yes, I hear you. I am a good little soldier. I *can* follow directions."

He sighed. "Don't be a twat."

I laughed. "Look at you, fucking nailing Briticisms."

"Fuck you."

Curtis said, "You'll be happy to know I have another little project to keep you busy tonight while you're cooling your jets for the meeting between Prochenko and McLean. Stellan Tusk has a piece of decryption technology that we need to recover before he sells it on the black market. You need to take a team and crash a little party he's having tonight, and I've sent all the details to your tablet. Call me back if you have any questions."

He hung up, and I dragged my sheets off. I could feel it. The adrenaline flood. It made me too edgy, too jumpy. I needed to calm my mind down and focus on the things I could control. Prochenko would be mine in a matter of days.

First, I'd calm down my mind, and then I'd calm down my

body with some exercise. And the number one thing guaranteed to zone me out mentally, to get me in that peaceful headspace, was cleaning my weapons.

You have strange hobbies.

I tried to ignore my internal peanut gallery. Then I went to the bookcase, opened up my concealed gun safe, and pulled out the weapons I'd need for that night.

In systematic fashion, I dismantled them, pulled out my cleaning tools and gun oil, and applied them on my guns like every absolutely normal government contractor.

But none of this is normal.

Once all my guns were clean and my go bag was out and ready to pack, there was a knock at the door. I figured it was probably Mrs. Washington with my newspaper. She liked to drop it off on my doorstep as she was always up early. She never came inside, so I didn't feel the need to hide everything away before I opened the door.

But when I yanked it open, I stopped short, surprised to find Lyra on my doorstep. And instead of letting the door swing wide, I held it only slightly ajar. "Are you okay? Is something wrong?" My primary alarms hadn't gone off.

"No, I'm fine." She held a bag of what smelled like sugary, fried deliciousness.

"What's all this?"

"This is me returning a favor. You got me breakfast, used your body as a human shield, and brought me dinner when I really needed it."

I checked her face. Her bruise was far less visible that morning. But just because I couldn't see it didn't mean I'd forgotten it was there.

"Your face looks better."

She shrugged. "Well, it's just good makeup."

"You don't look like you need it."

Her smile was tentative at first, but then her face broke into a larger grin. "You are good with flattery, Marcus Black."

She held up the doughnut bag and the coffee. "I assumed you would like it black."

I nodded slowly, reaching out through the door and using my foot to keep it from opening any farther. "Thank you."

She frowned slightly. "Um, are you busy coding or something?"

He nodded. "Yeah, uh, now is not a great time."

Her eyes went wide. "Okay, sorry. I guess I'll go finish getting ready for work. I just wanted to say thank you again for, you know, last night, and yesterday morning, and the other night, I guess."

For a woman who usually was so self-assured, she looked confused. Like I'd cut her off about something. "Well, you make the best wake up call."

She licked her lips, and I saw a dusting of sugar on one of the corners of her mouth. Just like last time, I reached out and wiped it off with my thumb. "You've got some sugar there."

Her breath caught, and my thumb hesitated. Christ. I wanted to kiss her. I really, really wanted to fucking kiss her. The pull was getting harder to ignore. Especially when her tongue reached out to lick the spot I'd brushed, and the tip flicked my thumb.

I thought I'd caught the sound of my moan before it could escape, before it could give me away. But I knew it had been audible, because her pupils dilated and she swayed a little. All I wanted to do was step back and let her in and then put the powdery, dusty doughnuts all over her tits and lick them. And I would have. Fuck, I would have just given in. But I had my guns all over the coffee table, and there was absolutely no reason Marcus Black the video game designer should have guns on his table. So I kept the door just slightly ajar and pulled my thumb back like I'd been scorched. "Well, thank you for breakfast."

Her brow furrowed slightly. "I, uh... Maybe one of these days we should do this properly at my place."

Oh fuck, she was trying to kill me. That's what this was. She was trying to kill me slowly with priapism. Wasn't that the thing where if your dick was hard for more than four hours, you were supposed to go to the ER? That's what she was doing to me. I tried to talk, but I couldn't because my voice was too hoarse. I tried it again. "Yeah, maybe some other time. I, um, you know, am working."

She nodded. "Oh, right. Of course, I'll just go get ready for work. I'll, uh, return your dish later. Thanks again, Marcus. Have a good day."

"Yeah, you too, Lyra."

I watched her walk into her flat, and I had to grip the doorframe to keep myself from going after her.

You do not have time for this. You have a mission. And until you catch Stannis, getting any closer to her just puts her in danger. Stand down, motherfucker.

I did not want to fucking stand down. But I forced myself backward, closed my door, and leaned my forehead against it. To be safe, I locked it.

Yeah, as if that will keep your dick locked in.

It would have to, because for the time being, I had bigger fish to fry.

8

LYRA

I wished I could explain the feeling that had come over me. The clawing, acrid, bitter bile in my throat. It felt like... *jealousy.*

Someone was in there with him.

I could tell. His caginess, the unwillingness to even open the door. Christ, was she naked and laid out on his coffee table?

Nope, I did not need to think about that. It wouldn't help. He was well within his rights to have someone over. We weren't a thing.

Weren't you the one who told him you didn't want to pursue anything?

That was until I saw him with someone else. Not that I'd *seen* anything. But I knew that he was hiding something in his apartment, and the only thing that made sense was another date.

If I really wanted to, I could find out who was in there. Do a little background check on her. Make sure she wasn't a psycho.

You *sound like a psycho.*

I did sound crazy. What the hell was wrong with me? It wasn't that I didn't want him; it was that I was trying to keep him out of the fray. Did he find someone else who wanted him more, or was it someone already in his life?

As I chomped on my own doughnut and took swigs of coffee while packing up for work, I called Addie. "Hey, can you get me eyes and ears on 5F West Harrison Street?"

Addie laughed. "Good morning to you too. Yes, and thank you for the coffee you're going to bring me after being in all night."

"Oh, sorry, I forgot that you weren't off last night."

"No, I wasn't. And you've got a job tonight."

I groaned. "Fine, brief me when I get in."

"Will do. But who are we spying on? That sounds like your address."

I wrinkled my nose. "It *is* my address, but it's Marcus's flat."

Addie laughed. "Oh no, we don't spy on civilians."

"We do if they're cheaters."

"A cheater?"

I sighed. "Fine, I'm not *dating* him, *per se*, but he kissed me. So if he's kissing me, why is he kissing other sexy women?"

Addie inhaled a deep breath as if she was preparing to talk, to explain something very complex to a small child. "Sweetheart, is this the same guy you swore to stay away from because it was too dangerous for him?"

"That's beside the point. If he's put himself in danger of catching a fucking STD from some hoe, then he's on his own."

Addie just laughed. "Calm your tits. You don't want him, remember?"

"I didn't say I didn't *want* him. I just said I can't *have* him." I stepped into my Stuart Weitzman stilettos.

"Look, you recognize that you sound jealous, right?"

"I'm not jealous. I just thought he meant it when he said he was into me."

She laughed then. "Yes, but didn't you say that he was boring?"

"That was *before* the kiss. If I'd known he could kiss like that, I'd have kissed him on the first date."

"The one that got interrupted by your mission?"

I frowned. "Okay fine, I would have kissed him on the second date."

"The one that got interrupted by his food poisoning?"

I tried to curb my impatience. "Addie, can you just do it? I just need ears in his place."

"Oh boy," she hooted. "You *do* like him."

"I do *not* like him. I am just concerned. You're hearing my voice of concern."

"Sure, it is. And no, I'm not going to spy on him. You have traffic cams pointed at his apartment, and you can check those yourself. I'm not logging in on that for you. Roz will shit a brick when she finds out that is your plan. And I'm assuming you don't want her up your ass about this."

"Fuck, no."

"Right. So, I'm not going to spy on him unless you think he needs to be spied on for some other reason. Do you think Prochenko has any reason to be after him?"

I laughed. "Marcus? No. He is your general good guy. Nothing special about Marcus except the way he kisses and the love affair he has with our elderly neighbor."

Addie laughed. "Rose?"

"Rose."

"I love that old lady. She's cool."

I chuckled. "You would, because that's who you're going to end up like when you're in your eighties."

"From your lips to God's ears," Addie agreed.

"Except, you'll have a lot more weapons."

"Hell yes, I will. Now get your ass in here. Mission brief in thirty minutes."

"I'm out the door now."

As I left, I tried to linger in the hallway, hoping to see whoever the hell was going to come out of his flat. But nothing happened.

I glanced at my watch. If I didn't get moving, I was going to be late.

You're not allowed to like him. Like someone else. You liking him isn't going to be good for his health.

Then I forced myself to get to work and to put thoughts of Marcus's piercing deep blue eyes out of my mind.

Lyra

Thirty minutes later during the mission briefing, Roz was pacing back and forth as she clicked buttons on the remote, showing our target for the night. "This mission is classified, so all I can give you are the basics. Our target is Stellan Tusk, and the goal is to acquire an important decryption device in his possession and get out without being discovered."

She turned back to her screen. "So here is the layout of the location where you'll be attending a party hosted by Tusk.

We've decided to send in a five-person team, and you should each have more details on your tablets."

She slid me a glance and asked. "Everyone understand?"

We all nodded, and she approached me with her arms crossed. "Are you okay? Any lingering effects from the last mission?" Her hand reached out to graze the bruise on my cheek.

It hurt a little, but I remained stoic. "It's not like it's my first time to be hurt like this. It's nothing, really. I am mission ready for tonight."

"I know. That's not what I mean. I just don't want Prochenko in your head. I don't think your mental health is compromised. I just want you to be careful and concentrate on the parameters of *this* mission."

"Thanks, Mom."

She laughed. "Okay, joke all you want, but I do care about you."

"I know. And I'm grateful. But I'm good. Prochenko came back for me, so when we finish this job, it's time for payback."

"Revenge isn't what we're after here, Lyra. We want answers."

"I know. Bring the man in alive. I got you."

"Good." Her smile was soft. "You look... I don't know, keyed up. Everything okay with your dating life?"

I rolled my eyes. "I know what you're fishing for. Nothing happened."

Roz opened her mouth to say something else, but I put up my hands and cut her off. "I know, I know. Find love. I'm working on it. But maybe after we deal with Prochenko, okay?"

She sighed. "Okay, but it's actually important. I'd rather

you start screwing someone than have to make extra appointments with the psych counselor."

I winced at that. I didn't need to see a psych just because I wasn't actively banging someone. "Like I said, I'm working on it. Now, can we deal with Tusk and then Prochenko first?"

"Yeah, let's get these assholes. No one comes after my agents."

"Excellent."

Then I left her and went back to my office. I had a brief to review, and I had to get ready for tonight. I could ignore my feelings about Marcus. I knew how to do my job, and there was no way I was letting him stand in my way.

But a quick double check of my weapons pack and tablet told me I'd left my special hairpins that assembled into knives at home. Christ. I'd been so preoccupied I'd left them on my coffee table.

Marcus Black was bad for my health and my sanity.

Lucky for me, I had time before the mission rolled out to go home and get my pins. I could always get another pack from the armory, but every weapons checkout was monitored. With Tyler back and throwing me off, I didn't need any extra attention on me.

I glanced up quickly. I had two hours. More than enough time.

~

MARCUS

I only heard Lyra come home as I was prepping for that night's mission because Mrs. Washington had her door opened and her voice was bright and sunny as she spoke.

"Lyra, you're back. Now, dear, I have a package for you. Hold on."

I jumped up, not like I'd been waiting for her or anything. *Who are you kidding? You want to see her.*

I opened my door. "Hi, Lyra."

She whirled around, cheeks flushed. "Oh, hey, Marcus." We both hesitated. But she spoke first. "Sorry about this morning. I didn't mean to interrupt. I know it was probably awkward. I just came to say that maybe I want to take you up on that dinner invitation. But obviously you were busy."

I studied her closely. What was her play here?

I narrowed my gaze. This was about what happened earlier. She thought I'd been with another woman. "Actually, I'm not free tonight."

She lifted a brow. "Well neither am I. I just forgot something that I needed, so I'm popping by to grab it before I go back out." She tried to look beyond me into my flat. "Busy? Doing what?"

"Just... busy."

She blinked slowly, her gaze never wavering from mine. "I didn't mean tonight." She shifted on her feet. "I have a work event." With a nervous lick of her lips she said, "You know, you confuse me. The other day you were practically begging me to go out with you again. This morning you were *occupied*," she said, using air quotes. "And now you're busy again. Are you ghosting me?"

I grinned at that. "I was just *busy* this morning, Lyra. There was no one else here."

Mrs. Washington approached with Nyla's box. "Here you are, dear."

"Oh, thank you, Rose. You're very thoughtful." Her voice was all saccharine sweet for our elderly neighbor.

"Of course, honey," she said, her tanned, leathery skin creasing as she smiled. "I do have to warn you that poor little Button did get into your packaging."

Was it my imagination, or did Lyra's normally vibrant brown skin take on a gray pallor? "W-what?"

"Yes, love. All that vibrating scared him something awful though. He must have accidentally turned it on, because that rabbit was wiggling all over the floor and it looked like it was chasing him." She clasped her hand to her chest. "It gave him such a fright, but I was able to grab it and repackage it for you. Good as new. I wanted to make sure you got it. I know how us girls have to take care of things from time to time."

It took all my years of training to school my expression into a placid and uninterested expression.

Lyra, on the other hand, looked frozen. Her face was plastered into a small smile, her eyes a little too wide, and her jaw too tight. And her skin was now almost pink, particularly in the cheeks. She was blushing.

Oh, this just kept getting better and better. If I was right, somewhere in that Amazon packaging lay a slightly used-by-Button vibrator. And all three of us knew it.

As pink as she was, Lyra recovered quickly. "Oh, thank you so much. It was meant to be a gag gift. But perhaps I'll get something else."

Lies. I could see it in the shift of her eyes. The slight press of her mouth. And all it made me want to do was show her exactly what to do with that vibrator.

Well, well, she didn't know how to lie. Excellent that she wasn't great at it, but at least she knew how to pull something out of her ass if necessary.

"Well, I'll just be going."

I stopped her. "What about dinner though?"

"I thought you were busy?"

I flashed her a grin. "Lyra Wilkinson, are you jealous? Do you want us to be something more than friends?"

"You know what? Never mind. You have a good night, friend."

"Right, friends. Except... Maybe you don't want to be friends?"

She gave me a light chuckle and then struggled with her keys in the lock. "I don't know what you're talking about."

I followed her to her flat. Mrs. Washington winked at me before she closed her door.

"Lyra, wait up."

She sighed. "Marcus, it's been a long day. I need to grab these press gift packs that were sent here instead of the office and head back out."

She looked tired, the strain evident around her mouth, and I wondered what was going on. "Look, I had some things going on this morning that meant I couldn't hang out or talk. But I *would* like to take you out again."

"Didn't we have this conversation? We're *friends*. And I believe you just turned me down for dinner."

"Right. Don't you go places with your friends?"

She frowned at that. "But see, we're not *just* friends, we're also neighbors."

"Okay, neighbors. But maybe neighbors who go out sometimes?"

Her lips twitched as if she was going to laugh, but she held it together.

"You're impossible."

"So you've told me." There was something in her dark eyes. A wariness maybe.

When she took a deep breath, I thought she was going to

remind me that her life was complicated. But she surprised me.

"Look, I was going to ask you this morning. I have tickets to the What is Love couples exhibit at The Venice in the City Bacchanal this coming weekend. Do you want to go with me?"

Fuck me.

I'd planned on asking someone anonymous to be my date. But she was standing in front of me asking me to do the one thing I really wanted to do, which was to be near her.

I hesitated a moment too long, and she said, "It's okay. You don't have to. I think I read this wrong." She turned to go.

I knew better, *knew* that this was going to be a bad idea, but I couldn't stop myself. "Wait, Lyra. I'd love to go with you."

She swallowed, hard. "Honestly, it's okay. You don't have—"

Danger, danger.

I knew having one taste wasn't going to be enough, but I did it anyway. I interrupted her with a kiss. By now our tongues had learned a shorthand. The slow slide, the teasing licks, and then the deep dive, losing ourselves in the taste, the smell, and the feel of each other.

I knew enough to wait for that whimper before fully pulling her in. That little acquiescence of her letting me know this was something she wanted more than anything.

Before I knew it, that sound came, and I dragged her to me, my hands cupping her ass. Pulling her straight up against me, I turned her body and angled her in the door frame. I didn't give a fuck who saw. Whether Mrs. Washington or any of the other neighbors were watching from their door, I didn't care. I couldn't *not* taste her. I couldn't *not* have her.

This was what I'd wanted to do that morning, drag her body against mine and relive that kiss that had been interrupted.

I poured everything I had into kissing her. Bending my knees slightly so I could angle her better. My hands fisted in her hair that she'd pulled back into a low bun. Gently, I tugged the pins that held it in place and set her locks free. I ran my fingers my fingers through it, knowing I was probably making it a mess, but I didn't get give a fuck.

Her hands slid up my chest, her delicate fingers sliding then depressing as if trying to pull at my shirt to get to my skin. And then her hands came up to my face and gently rubbed over the stubble before sliding into my hair at the nape of my neck. When her nails scored over the skin on my scalp, I growled.

Hands digging into her ass, I picked her up just a little. So enough that she could feel just how much I wanted her, how much I *needed* her. And then the buzzing was skipping up my spine and I couldn't think. Like my brain had been taken over by some kind of feral animal, and all I wanted to do was take and plunder and—

There was more buzzing along the length of my dick, and I barked out a cough.

Bollocks. I dragged my lips off of hers as I realized that the buzzing wasn't an impending orgasm, though one of those had been chasing me down too. It was her phone in her pocket.

I set her down gently and made myself take a deliberate step back. "I'm sorry."

She stood there shaking her head for a moment and slowly dragged her eyes open, her dark chocolate gaze meeting mine. "You should be sorry. All this time, you could have been kissing me like that."

I grinned at her. "You probably need to get that."

"W-what?"

"Your phone. It's ringing."

Her eyes went wide. "Oh shit." She grabbed for her phone, and then answered it. "Yep, I'll be right there. I just needed something from my apartment." When she hung up, her gaze skittered back to mine. "I have to go."

I nodded slowly, desperate to rearrange my jeans so she wouldn't be able to tell just how badly I was tenting them. But moving at all would mean I'd be moving in her direction, and that was a bad call right now. I had a mission to get ready for, but instead, all I could think about was sliding into her hot sweet depths and spending days exploring her body.

I cleared my throat and said, "I should let you go."

"Yes." She waved her phone. "This is me going. I will see you later, I guess." She turned to walk into her apartment, but then she paused and turned to look at me. And when she started walking again, she narrowly missed the wall.

I knew I was wearing a shit-eating grin. But I couldn't help it. Lyra Wilkinson was under my skin. In my blood. I didn't just want her, I *liked* her. Which was why I was so worried that I'd said yes to attending the Bacchanal with her.

But I would have to do everything in my power to keep her safe. Not going with her wasn't an option now, so I would have to figure out how to protect her.

9

LYRA

The mission was simple. Or was *supposed* to be simple. All we had to do was steal the decryption device. The problem was that it was in one of the most secure vaults belonging to one of the most dangerous men in the Northern Hemisphere. Stellan Tusk, a wealthy South African with investments in everything from oil to gold to NFTs.

He was also a very bad boy and like so many criminals before him, he was greedy. He liked to add to his wealth by selling weapons, drugs, and black-market goods. In this case, a top-secret decryption device that had been stolen from the NSA. It was a prototype and was purported to open any digital device given enough input.

Tusk was well protected. He had a personal team of six bodyguards that were never more than mere feet away from him and an additional guard force around the house of six to twelve more, depending on the occasion. The only side of his estate that wasn't heavily guarded was the beach access route.

The cliffs and caves below and a private beach with only a slim lane of stairs along the edge made it easily defensible.

The only way to get close to him was his dick. He liked women. *Lots* of women. *All kinds* of women. The more the merrier, usually naked and subservient to him, because that was the only way he liked his women, not with clothes and opinions. He met them mostly via parties, lots of escorts and party girls. His parties were invitation only, and lucky us, we'd secured an invitation.

"Status report." Tyler's voice was cold, crisp, and as irritating as tinnitus after a loud concert.

I ground my teeth as I scowled at Addie. "Does he have to be on this?"

She rolled her eyes. Tyler was our comms man on the mission, and I'd been clenching my jaw so tight I was sure I'd have TMJ after this.

Our five-person team consisted of Addie and I inside, Tyler on comms, Kira as our sniper, and then there was Luke, our wet works specialist, posing as a waiter. Even though we didn't expect trouble on this mission, we were lucky because he was one of the deadliest operatives I'd ever seen in hand-to-hand combat, and no one attending the party was allowed to have a weapon.

"Jesus Christ, it's like a buffet. Pick your mark."

Addie laughed. "Yes, well, these things are usually like that, and hey, at least it's not an auction block."

I shuddered. "You know, I'm going to thank God for small favors."

She chuckled. "Remember when we broke up that sex trafficking ring last year? Selling young women against their will. At least these women are being compensated."

I shook my head. "God, fucking human traffickers are

pure filth." Those kinds of missions always made my trigger finger itchy.

She shrugged. "I mean, hey, if a girl wants to take charge of her own virginity and sell it herself, fine. I'm all for it. Fuck the patriarchy, sister."

"I know. But for most of those other women, that wasn't the case. Kidnapped, bought and sold, that shit makes me crazy."

"Guys like Stellan here, he just brings escorts to him. All these girls were told there was a hot party and they'd get to meet a billionaire. He pays for everything, their dresses, their jewels, and they get to keep it, even if they're not selected for the night. Wouldn't you come back?"

I shrugged. "Yeah, I guess so."

Over the comms, Kira muttered, "All right, he's on his way. Lyra, you're up. Addie you're on support."

I took my champagne and attempted to smile sweetly.

With firm strides, I filtered my way through the crowd.

Just outside of what appeared to be the kitchen doors, there was a balcony to the left, then a side door that led to Stellan's private chambers toward the back of the house. Thanks to our inside man, we knew his exact movements because he'd had a tracker placed on him.

"And three, two, one."

I opened the door and then teetered on my heels, accidentally on purpose.

"Oh, be careful."

Firm hands gripped my elbows, and I had to tamp down a shudder of revulsion when he touched me. "Oh my God, I'm so sorry. I don't know what happened. I guess I'm not used to wearing heels."

He smiled down at me. "I haven't seen you here before."

"Oh, I'm new. I hope it's okay that I came. A girlfriend invited me."

He lifted a brow. "Which girlfriend?"

Every single person who attended the party was vetted before being approved for the guest list. One of his regular girls was one of our agents. "Oh, my friend Megan, Megan Campbell. She said it would be okay to come along. She gave my name and everything."

The tension around his mouth eased. "Oh, Megan. Dark hair, right?"

I nodded and gave him a tentative smile. "She says she always has fun here, and your house is beautiful."

What the hell else did you say to someone to sound simpering? I had no idea.

Behind me, Addie called loudly. "There you are."

She lurched forward, acting slightly drunk. "Oh my God, I'm so glad I found you. Where did you go? We girls have to stick together, right?"

Stellan nodded at one of his men, but I wrapped an arm around her protectively. "I'm sorry. We met at the bar. I think she's had too much. Is there somewhere she could lie down or something?"

Stellan tipped his head to one of his men. "We'll put her in a car and send her home."

"No, no. I mean, I wouldn't want her banned or anything. I think, honestly, your bartender has a really heavy hand. She only had the one drink."

His brow furrowed. "Who is she? I haven't seen her before."

"I don't even know her. I think her name's Crystal or something."

He studied me closely, and I just blinked up at him

owlishly, doing my very best wide-eyed innocent act. He said, "Your skin is quite remarkable. You should never wear makeup."

What the fuck? "Oh, yeah. I don't usually wear much, just the eye makeup and stuff. I was blessed with good skin."

Lies. I was wearing at least a pound of it to cover up that fucking bruise. At least the eye hadn't gone full black, but my cheek hurt. But he couldn't see it, because to him it looked like I had an excellent dot of highlighter on. "Do you think Crystal can lie down a minute? I know you're a private person, but I don't trust sending her off on her own."

I held my breath for a long moment before he finally said, "Right. Come along."

I hid my relief and followed Tusk. A massive bodyguard walked in front of him, and another followed behind me and a seemingly drunk Addie. He showed us to a massive room. A giant bed stood on the far wall in the center. There was a sitting area and what looked to be an insane closet. "Wow, this guest room is nice."

He laughed. "This is anything but a guest room."

"What, this is your room? Oh. I don't think she needs to rest in here. I figured a guest room would be fine."

"Never let it be said that I don't take care of my guests."

Addie teetered on over to one of the couches and flopped down.

She shoved her hand up in her hair and started scratching her scalp. "Oh my God, I'm so drunk. What was in that drink? I felt fine just a minute ago. Do you think he did something to my drink?"

Her eyes went wide, and I studied Stellan. "You don't think that would happen, do you?"

He shook his head. "No. Not my men. They've all been vetted."

Except, his usual bartender hadn't been available, thanks to us. He'd had to call the service, and we'd sent him one of ours.

"You don't think... I hope he's not hurting any other girls. Maybe it was just a heavy drink. What do I know?"

A muscle in Stellan's jaw ticked. One thing we knew about him was that he *hated* traffickers. He and his sister had been stolen from their home in South Africa and sold. He had escaped, but his sister had not. He might be a weapons dealer, and he might sell drugs, the kind that would kill millions. But he didn't traffic in human beings, and the idea clearly made him ill.

I played into it and looked down at my poor friend, 'Crystal.' I stroked her hair back, surreptitiously handing her one of the pins from my hair that would complete the little knife she would eventually have in her hand. "You're going to be okay," I said reassuringly.

Stellan muttered to one of his guards. "Check on the bartender. If any of the girls look ill or like they've had too many, even though there's a two-drink maximum, make sure they all get put into cars then are taken directly home. I want confirmation, you hear me?"

His guard nodded. The other one remained in place. Stellan laughed. "You don't need to stay. These two are harmless."

Those were my favorite words in moments like this. His second guard left, and Stellan approached. He leaned down over 'Crystal.' "I've seen you before, right?"

She smiled sloppily. "I'm a guest of Veronica's."

He nodded. "Ah yes, Veronica. She did say she was

bringing one of the girls from the restaurant where she works."

Addie shook her head. "I'm not from the restaurant. I'm her masseuse." Addie passed his little test with ease.

He grinned. "Ah yes, my mistake."

That wasn't a mistake. I knew it, and Addie knew it. He was testing her. He didn't trust her. Which made things a little more complicated.

I stepped forward. "Well, thank you, Mr. Tusk. You can go if you want. We won't take anything. Take my purse and hold it if you want, but I'll just sit with her if you don't mind."

His gaze on me was steady. "Why did you want to come to the party tonight?"

"Well, I don't know. My friend said it would be fun. I just went through a breakup, and I wanted to do something interesting and exciting, I guess."

"Well my parties are definitely exciting."

He took my hand, pulling me closer to him. "You really do have the most incredible skin." His thumb traced over my opposite cheek, the one that wasn't bruised.

I held his gaze, biting my bottom lip. "Do you do this with all the girls?"

"Well, I like my women to come to me. I rarely leave my house. And I always select the best women."

Gag me. "Oh yeah? What makes me the best?"

"Your skin, your smile."

I dipped my gaze low, my finger gently roaming over one of the rounded bulbs on the clasp of my purse. I peeled off the adhesive with my nail and then gently slid my hand up his torso to his neck, right under his ear. I brought my nail against his skin, displacing the adhesive, and smiled up at him as I ran my hand through his hair. "Why did you pick me?"

"Didn't I already answer that?"

"Yes, my skin, my smile, whatever. But why did you really *pick* me?"

He shrugged. "You looked real. Unlike the plastic girls that are in there, you seem like you might actually be a person. And sometimes that's what we're all looking for, a little connect—" He frowned. "I..." He shook his head and frowned again. "Sorry. You're just..." He glanced down at his glass.

I stepped back. "What's wrong?"

"I fear I may have the same affliction that your friend does. Suddenly, I don't feel well."

He opened his mouth to call out, and I brushed my fingers over his lips. "Oh, no, no, no, no. Just lie down. I'll help you."

I took his hand as he wove toward the bed. When he leaned his weight onto me, I almost collapsed, but I kicked off my shoes and helped him to the bed. "Oh God. Fuck, is this okay? Are you okay?"

He nodded, blinking rapidly, trying to clear his head. The sedative was powerful. It was only absorbed when it came in contact with human skin, which was why I'd used my nail to peel it off. He started to call out again, and I leaned over him. "No need for that. I can help you. Do you need water? I'll get you water."

I started to turn, but he pulled on my hand. "No, no. You stay."

He slowly blinked, and then he was out.

I held my breath as I checked his pulse. He was breathing and his pulse was good. I snapped my fingers and then checked his pupils. When I was satisfied, I tapped my comm unit. "He's out."

Addie was up in a flash. She had taken the pins from her hair and mine, and made a makeshift knife. That was the only weapon we were getting, so if anyone came through that door, she'd have to make it work. It was the only shot we had.

My job was to find the safe.

That proved slightly more difficult.

If I were a safe, where the fuck would I be?

There was one behind a painting in the main room, but when I checked the schematics, it wasn't the one we were looking for.

Addie checked the curtains. "Any luck?"

I shook my head. "Nothing."

And then I took a closer look inside his closet and said, "Hold on." I moved aside a rack of his dress shirts and hit pay dirt.

I tapped my comm unit and said, "Tyler, I'm here. What do we have?"

"Okay, grab your phone and turn on the app I put on it."

"Okay, done."

"All right, keep the app pointed at the safe and let it run the encryption."

"What's it doing?"

"Well, it's checking the pattern of fingerprints, the ones that have been touched most often, and it's cross-referencing them with things we know about Stellan. It's going to pull up the access code for you."

"Are you kidding me? What if it guesses wrong?"

"The encryption device we're stealing is one we already have. We just don't want anyone else to have it."

I laughed. "Of course."

Within seconds, I had the code and typed it in. Holding my breath, praying to God that this worked, I turned the handle. I waited for an alarm, bracing myself for hell to rain down, but nothing happened. It opened, and inside the safe, I found files, money, and many passports. I didn't have much time, but I quickly photographed each of the passports because it would give us a way to track Tusk's movements if he traveled under an alias.

Then I grabbed the device, put everything back the way I found it, wiped down the keypad, and closed it up before rearranging the shirts exactly how I'd found them.

I came running out of the closet, only pausing to grab my shoes. I checked on Stellan and found he was still out cold.

Addie nodded her head at me. "You have it?"

I nodded. "Yep. Let's go."

But as we ran for the door, the power went out.

Addie's voice was sharp. "Tyler, what the fuck?"

"It's not us. Get out of there."

We ran for the door, surprised to find that there was no guard. Then we heard gunshots down the hall. Hurriedly, we barricaded ourselves back in the room and ran for the balcony. "Fuck, Tyler, do we have an exit?"

"Back stairs on the balcony. The gardens are open and clear, but we've got company in the house."

"What the fuck do you mean 'company'?" I asked as we ran to the balcony.

Then a litany of swears came over the comms, and from the roof Kira muttered under her breath, "It looks like fucking Exodus. Retreat."

"Who has the decryption device?" Tyler asked.

I piped up. "I've got it."

"Only Lyra on the primary exit route then. Everyone else on secondary," said Tyler. His voice was stony and cold.

Addie stared at me. "What the fuck is going on?"

"I don't know. What the fuck is Exodus doing here? Aren't they in bed with assholes like this?" Had Exodus come to clean house?

She quickly motioned that she was switching to B channel, and I followed suit.

"What's up?"

"I was looking into why Tyler's here, due to my general mistrust of assholes."

She navigated barefoot down the ancient, narrow wooden stairs that led to the beach. It was eerily quiet out there. None of the guards were around.

"Addie, you know you're going to get slapped for doing that."

She shrugged. "I don't care. He doesn't matter right now. But listen, on the last six missions he's been on, Exodus has shown up for at least four of them and interrupted, tried to take a target that we were going after. Something's going on."

I frowned. "Do you think Exodus came to clean house?"

Exodus. The Firm had a history with them. We all used to be one organization. The original founders, Aidan Saint-James and Orion McClintock, were the best of friends, former spec ops, and wanted to change the world. Together, they founded a covert organization that could take care of the scum of the earth. But at some point, they diverged over their philosophies of how exactly that should be done and had a falling out. As a result, Aidan Saint-James kept The Firm, and Orion McClintock formed Exodus. But rumor was that Exodus went dirty and became hit men for hire. What were they doing on our jobs?

"I don't know. We'll find out, but be safe."

At the bottom of the stairs, I started sprinting left, and she went right. Neither one of us said goodbye. We knew the rules. We just switched back to the main comm channel and bolted.

As I sprinted for the boat, shoes in my hand and the decryption device shoved in my bra, I glanced back up at the house on top of the hill and saw someone running. They had a long, strong gait, and their gun was aimed at me.

I started running in a zigzag pattern, waiting for the bullets to rain down, but they didn't.

He was waiting for something. *What?*

I turned back. The sun had already begun to set, making the sky a light purple hue. I frowned because there was something familiar about him, but that wasn't one of our uniforms. We tended to favor black leather, with a tighter black jacket, but he was wearing tactical cargo pants and jacket.

He was Exodus.

But he still didn't shoot.

I climbed into the boat, taking care to make sure that my wig was on correctly after the long sprint. If I couldn't straighten my hair, I wore a wig. The last thing we needed was anyone recognizing me because of my Afro or my curls. I started the engine and turned back to make sure the Exodus agent wasn't coming after me. He wasn't. He just stood there, staring.

I tapped my comm unit. "I have the device, and I'm coming in."

Tyler's voice was satisfied. "Copy, I'll meet you at the rendezvous point."

"Roger."

I couldn't shake the feeling. I knew that Exodus agent...
but from where?

~

MARCUS

"On your mark."

I checked the scope. My target was a woman with long,
flowing dark hair. She was getting in a boat.

"I see a target escaping at the north side of the beach.
Already in the boat."

"Do you have a shot?"

That was the tricky part. From this distance and with the
right wind, I could probably hit her.

But something itched over my skin every time my finger
moved to the trigger. I had a long-range rifle. I could take the
shot.

At least try.

I couldn't do it though. I knew female agents were just as
deadly as the male ones. Hell, I worked with many of them
that I wouldn't want to cross. But there was something about
that woman. She was familiar, like an echo I already knew.

She reminded me of someone.

Simone.

Simone Bellevue had been my fiancée and also an agent.
We'd been stationed in Paris together. When my mission in
Prague hadn't ended well, I'd been shot pretty badly. She'd
come to see me at the safe house. Rhodes had arranged it.

But we were ambushed, and someone had killed Simone
that night. She'd thrown her body over me, and they'd made
a clean kill shot. I hadn't been able to protect her when they
had come for me.

Rhodes and the rest of the team took them out. I had never really recovered from losing her. Because of love, she'd come for me and paid with her life. I'd never been able to shake that feeling of helplessness. And that was four years ago.

"Agent Black, report."

I dragged my attention back to the task at hand and pressed the comm unit. "Already gone. I'm heading back to the house."

"Copy."

As I ran back, still unable to shake the lingering familiarity of the woman on the beach, I asked, "What's the status of the device?"

"We're working on getting in the safe now."

"I want to see that guest list."

"Copy, it'll be here when you get back." As I headed toward the house, the hairs on the back of my neck refused to relax. What was it about that agent?

I made a mental note to go through a catalog of our most wanted. Maybe that's why she seemed familiar. I hadn't been able to see her face, but there was something about the way she ran. She'd moved like a dancer, lithe, easy, athletic. Still, my skin itched just thinking about her. I wanted to know who the fuck she was. When I reached the house, I found Rhodes in the master bedroom. Tusk was seemingly passed out.

"Are we going to revive him?"

Rhodes shook his head. "No, he's completely out of it. A little too conveniently because getting into the safe is tricky now."

"And the rest of the house guests?" Tusk had been throwing some kind of party.

"When the shooting started, everybody scattered. We're

already tapped into local police. We have three minutes before their arrival. We already dispatched all of Tusk's security team. What's your assessment?"

The Firm had beat us here again. The woman had been with them, but had they gotten what they came for?

Rhodes snapped his fingers in front of my face. "Hey, Earth to Marcus. What's going on with you?"

"I don't know. Something doesn't feel right. If this was The Firm, I caught sight of one of their agents running off along the beach. It's like I knew her."

He lifted a brow. "You recognized her?"

I shook my head. "No. She was too far away, but she was so fucking familiar. I can feel it."

He looked at me quizzically. "You're not making any sense, man."

"Fuck, I can't explain it. Just trust me."

Rhodes blew out a low breath. "All right, if you think you know her, after debriefing go through some footage. Maybe we'll get lucky."

Neither one of us believed in luck.

One of the decryption techs finally sent a text that hit our tablets.

Rhodes tapped in the key he gave us, and we prayed. I checked my watch. We only had forty-five seconds. "We've got to go. This place is about to be crawling with police."

Rhodes nodded. "I hear you."

He got the safe open and searched inside. All he found were passports, money, jewels. Nothing of interest.

He cursed under his breath. "We have a problem. I repeat, we have a problem. The device is missing."

And I knew the woman on the beach had taken what I'd come there to collect.

Lyra

Once back at The Firm headquarters, I couldn't shake the feeling or the intensity I'd felt from the man on the bluffs.

My brain was still trying to lock onto any detail that might help me identify him as I took the decryption device to tech and headed down to the conference room for debriefing.

I was sore and achy, and all I wanted to do was crawl into my own damn bed. But the debriefing came first. I eased down into one of the conference room chairs, the normally smooth leather feeling like sandpaper on my raw nerves.

When Roz walked in, she did not look pleased.

Her piercing baby blue gaze said everything, and in my head, I heard her voice asking what she'd not yet said with her mouth. *What the fuck happened on that mission?*

In reality, she spoke only one word. My name. It was clipped and businesslike. Roz was not there to play. "Lyra?"

I understood her confusion. I had my own in spades. "I don't know what happened. I retrieved the device from the safe. Addie was watching my back. Once we had the device, we went to the door for egress as planned. But there was no guard. Then we heard shooting, so we went to the secondary point of egress. As you can hear on the comms recording, we have no idea what went on inside the house. We were just as blind as you were."

She turned her attention to Tyler then. "You were on over watch. How the hell did Exodus know we were there?"

He shook his head. "I don't know. The mission was airtight. It should have been an easy in and out. But they must have been after the device too, which means someone has been feeding them intel." He shrugged. "Or maybe it was a deal gone wrong with Tusk himself. But they came fully armed, so they were expecting trouble, which would hardly have been the case if they'd had a deal with Tusk."

Roz leaned her hands on the desk and pinned each of the five of us with her glare. "I want this buttoned up. Exodus has shown up on one too many of our missions. They know our moves before we do, so we need to figure out why. I'm concerned they're going to show up on the Stannis Prochenko mission as well, because right now, they are too much of a constant presence. And they seem to be one step ahead of us. I want it locked down. Tyler, you're in charge."

I almost started to argue, but I was too tired, and Tyler was technically the senior agent. I hated it, but it was true. Besides, we had a common goal. If Exodus was trying to infiltrate our missions, they were up to something. The question was, what?

Roz crossed her arms. "We do have another problem. The Bacchanal organizers have asked for a guest list. Couples or throuples. They are being very inclusive in that respect, but absolutely no singles are allowed. You are going to need to look the part. So I'm going to assign—"

I knew what she was going to say. I was about to get paired with Tyler. And no way no how was that going to work for me, so I piped up with something outlandish. "Do you think the fair and the exhibit are a smokescreen? The artist's brother has ties with Victus. She's never been associated directly, but he's her half-brother. If it's a smokescreen, no doubt they'll be vetting all the guests. We should pair with civilians if we can."

Roz lifted a brow. "Go on."

If we do some civilian pairings, especially since the nature of the event is geared toward couples, it would be really suspicious if two of us vanish at once. But if one of us needs to sneak off for a 'bathroom break' while we're paired with a civilian, it will look completely natural. No red flags."

"That's an interesting idea. I can set it up. We have some civilian marketing partners."

I started to breathe a little easier. At least that meant I wouldn't be stuck with Tyler, and I'd already set it up to go with Marcus.

But that would put him in danger. Right in the crosshairs.

But while I was worrying about Marcus's safety, Tyler was trying to get his digs in. "While this whole couples thing might actually be a real problem we have, let's face it; Lyra just wants to take her new boyfriend on a mission, like it's show and tell or something."

Addie, ever loyal, chimed in. "Tyler, don't be jealous. It's not becoming. Marcus may be a civilian, but he lives and works in the community. He'll provide Lyra with a good cover."

Roz was nodding. Why was she nodding? This was a terrible idea. All I wanted was to avoid Tyler. I hadn't meant to drag Marcus into it, but there might not be an easy way out of this one since I'd already asked him, and Roz appeared to think it was a great idea.

"Right. I think Lyra's partner is settled. It looks good, and he'll be an easy-access pass. Tyler, we'll need to find you someone above reproach. Perhaps the local librarian. Addie and Kira, same goes for both of you. We'll make it work." She then turned her attention back to me. "Good call, Lyra. Smart thinking."

As Roz walked out of the briefing room, Tyler turned to me and scowled. "If your boyfriend fucks this up, I get to shoot him. And trust me, I've been looking forward to that."

10

LYRA

I was a nervous wreck on Saturday night. What the hell had possessed me to drag Marcus into this?

You have to look out for him. Try and keep him safe.

My team was in the field. It would be all right. I checked my appearance in the mirror one more time, hardly recognizing the woman I saw. This woman's eyes were wide, her cheeks flushed. She looked excited. Preparing for the mission this week had left me very little personal time, so I hadn't seen much of Marcus. This was all far more complicated than I had bargained for.

I'd opted for an outfit that I could move in. A skirt, showing my legs, but paired with breathable flats, a plain white T-shirt, and a slim-fit leather jacket to hide all my weapons.

I kept my hair simple, leaving it curly. Besides, I didn't have time to fiddle with it. When I'd originally thought my partner was going to be Addie or Tyler, I hadn't planned to take time to bother with it. Now that it was an actual date with Marcus, I wanted to look better, but given the lack of prep time, natural was as good as it got.

When the knock sounded, I took a deep breath before I opened the door. Marcus stood on the other side looking like he'd just walked off of a magazine shoot. He was holding a bouquet of flowers and wearing dark wash jeans, partially unlaced black boots, a light blue sweater that matched his eyes, and a comfortable looking leather jacket on top. His hair was this sort of messy, wild disarray of dark curls that I wanted to run my fingers through. The man looked good enough to eat, and he knew it.

"Hi."

His gaze swept in on my frame, those ice blue eyes growing darker. "Jesus, you look amazing."

I grinned. "Thank you. You brought me flowers?"

"Yeah. I remembered these were your favorite."

I frowned at that. Had I told him that? Then I remembered as we'd walked to the restaurant on one of our dates, I'd mentioned my mother always had lilacs when I was growing up.

The sting behind my eyes surprised me, and I said, "Oh wow, that's so sweet of you."

"One of these days, you're going to stop calling me sweet."

My brain remembered that he wasn't sweet at all. The way he'd kissed me a few days earlier was like a man who knew how to possess me heart and soul. "You know that's not a bad thing, right?"

"I thought women like men with a little more edge."

She shook her head. "No. Not all women." *Lies. You like his edge.*

"Right."

"Let me get these in a vase and then we can go."

Before walking outside, Marcus took my hand, pulling me to him. "I'm going to go crazy if I don't do this first."

The kiss was quick, hot, and made my knees buckle inside of three seconds. When he pulled back, all I could do was attempt to bring my sanity back online.

Outside of the flat, Marcus led me toward a sleek black sportscar and opened the door for me. I frowned. "Is this you?"

He laughed. "Yes, it is. Normally when we have a date, we walk or we meet somewhere. But I wanted this to be a real date, so I'm trying to make a good impression."

The leather interior still had that new-car smell. "You must rarely drive this thing."

"You're right. I work primarily from home, so I don't get to use it often. But I do love it."

"I never would have figured you for a gearhead."

"There's a lot you don't know about me, Lyra Wilkinson."

"Maybe I'll find out more."

"Here's hoping you do."

The drive downtown wasn't a particularly long one, but I was glad I had my jacket to keep me from freezing in the T-shirt I'd worn. His gaze slid over me as I put on my seat belt. "You think you'll be warm enough? I can put the top up."

"No, I think I'll be fine." The air whipped around us as we started to drive, and I knew my curls would probably be tangled beyond measure, but I loved the freedom of the wind blowing and I didn't want it to stop. His gaze swept over me one more time, and I laughed as I pulled my hair back. "This is perfect."

"Good. I want you to have fun."

And I was. With him looking at me like this and the wind

blowing, I could almost believe this was real. That this was a feeling I could keep.

~

Lyra

The Bacchanal was eighteen and over because some of the images in the special exhibit contained nudity. But mostly, it was wholesome and fun. We came upon a particular image that was really stunning. He was holding my hand when we saw it, and all I could do was stand and stare. Marcus stopped as well and grinned.

I couldn't help the wistful sigh that came out. "Oh my God, that's a beautiful photo."

"Yes, yes, it is."

His hand was firm and warm, and we laughed and chuckled as he talked to me about the photos and paintings that particularly caught our attention. He also talked about his workday coding games and told me stories about his family and his nephew, and I couldn't help but see bits and pieces of him falling into place.

The more I saw, the more I wanted him. He had no idea that his voice, his mere presence even, were like a tease to me. Like a caress that I never wanted to stop.

Oh, you've got it bad.

The Bacchanal was a feast for the eyes. They decorated the desert to the east to look just like Venice. I'd heard from the planning committees that they'd even created canals. It was like we'd suddenly been transported into the 16th century. There were people in masquerade costumes and others who were dressed like us. Everywhere we looked there was light and color and couples and groups laughing and talking and dancing.

My favorite part was that there were also fair games. So many of them. They'd also set up a Ferris wheel and what looked like maybe a tilt-a-whirl. And then there were the exhibits. Interesting sculptures all around, depicting people in wild positions. There were also many pop-up galleries featuring up-and-coming painters and photographers. What I loved was that the work was priced anywhere from five dollars to fifty thousand dollars. It was the true spirit of art.

Marcus held my hand easily. And even though I kept my eyes peeled, I could relax until ten o'clock, as that was the time of the meeting between Stannis and the arms broker. But for the next hour and a half, I could be free.

We people-watched as we walked and talked. At one point, as he watched a couple in front of us start making out, Marcus chuckled and said. "They have the right idea."

The couple in front of us could barely keep their hands off each other. At one point the guy dragged his girlfriend into the darkness, and they started making out like a couple of teenagers.

But instead of Marcus following their lead, he just looped an arm around my shoulder and held me tight as we walked, sharing our cotton candy. "So, are you going to tell me about that guy?"

I frowned. "What guy?"

"Your ex. The one I met when I walked you to work. How long were you guys a thing?"

When in doubt, it is better to let your lie mirror the truth. "Only about four months. It was one of those things that was supposed to be temporary, but I didn't know."

"What does that mean?"

"Just that I was young and impressionable and didn't know any better. Didn't recognize all the signs of someone who was only using me for sex. One day he decided that he'd had enough and kicked me to the curb. I did not take it well."

"Shit, Lyra. I'm sorry. He's a dick."

I couldn't help but laugh. "Oh, I know."

"And what, you haven't been with anyone else since?"

How was I supposed to explain to him that when you worked for a secret government organization there wasn't really a lot of time for dating? "Nothing serious. What about you?"

He hesitated and pulled off a piece of cotton candy before plopping it in his mouth and leading me over to the fountains. Then he took a seat and pulled me into his lap on top of him. "I was engaged once."

I held myself perfectly still, waiting for the pain of the words to sink in. "Oh. For how long?"

"Three years. She died."

Damn it. The jealousy had been burrowing under my skin and trying to take root. But how could you be jealous of a woman who was gone? One that he clearly missed. "I'm so sorry, Marcus. How did it happen?"

"It was an accident. But I kind of see that I've been holding myself back ever since. Living a partial existence. But then I met you, and everything seemed normal. Something about you makes me want to open up. Be different."

I studied him. "You haven't been in love with anyone else since she died?"

He shook his head slowly. "No. Apparently, it took someone running after a mugger and attacking him with her shoes to get my attention. I know it sounds ridiculous, but watching you that night, it was the first time I'd felt alive in a while."

"Are you sure that's not just the adrenaline talking?"

"I'm sure. The point is that you're so different than what I thought I needed or wanted. But I like you. And you are 100% under my skin."

I flushed with warmth. I wanted him. I was also terrified. What if I got this wrong? "I lied, Marcus."

He gave me his fake shocked face, mouth hanging open and hand on his chest. "You don't say. What about, pray tell?"

I narrowed my gaze at him. He was going to make me use the words and say it out loud.

Maybe it's important that we hear them.

"I don't want to be your friend. I want to be more than your friend, and it scares the shit out of me."

That was probably the most honest thing I'd ever said to him, and as a result, I couldn't look him in the eyes for fear of what I would see in those icy blue depths.

But then he put a finger under my chin and lifted so I would have to meet his gaze. "You don't have to be scared. I'm not going to let anything hurt you."

I knew where this was going, into those feelings that I didn't want to examine too closely, so I cleared my throat and said, "Do you want to go on one of the rides?"

He grinned at me. "It depends on what you mean by ride."

I couldn't help it. All I could do was blink. And then I heard this low rumbling laugh that I realized was his. And as he laughed, dimples peeked out. Holy hell, he had dimples. Why had I never noticed before?

He said, "Oh my God, you should see your face."

"Don't tease me."

"Sweetheart, I haven't even started yet. Besides, what the hell do you think you're doing to me with that outfit?"

"I am merely enticing."

"If you say so. Come on. To the Ferris wheel?"

"Yes, please."

To our left, revelers were climbing on a makeshift gondola designed to take them on a little canal around the party area. I tried not to think about the amount of water that was being wasted, but I remembered that the event planners insisted the water would be put to good use, post revelry.

As Marcus's thumb stroked my hand, he asked, "After this, do you want to check out the main gallery? The artist... What's her name?"

"Nicola Wessex. I don't know a lot of her work, but I know she tries to push the boundaries of sexual conventions. Should be interesting at least."

Lyra

We climbed into the swinging car that had come to a stop in front of us.

I didn't realize at first that there were little monitors banked in the front of the Ferris wheel right below the bars where they locked us in.

I slid in first, then Marcus followed. Once we were locked in and started moving, the screen turned on. What we saw had my eyes growing wide and my palms going damp. A couple appeared on screen. The setting was the rooftop of some fabulous place somewhere. Fancy, with an infinity pool and a gorgeous city in the distance. You could also see the ocean in the distance with the clear azure water that could have been the Mediterranean or the Caribbean.

And then the couple on screen started kissing, and it wasn't long before their clothes started to come off.

My mouth fell open, and Marcus chuckled. "Well, I see they're taking the theme quite far."

I kept glancing down at Marcus's hand on my thigh, then my gaze would flick to the screen and back to his hand and back again. If this ride was twenty minutes long like the video display indicated, I was doomed. There was no way I would be able to survive. As it was, one little kiss from him and I was ready to jump out of my skin. Twenty minutes in this kind of close proximity with porn playing in front of us, and I knew spontaneous combustion could be a real thing. On the screen, I noticed the guy was surprisingly handsome for a porn guy. Not that I'd seen lots of porn guys.

Who are you kidding? Of course you have.

I squirmed in my seat. Marcus started to shift next to me as well. I wanted to look anywhere but at the screen or at him.

When he spoke, his voice was all gravel and cement. "Some fair warning would have been nice."

I shifted in place. "We don't have to watch. I wish we could turn it off or talk or something."

He chuckled. "Somehow, I can't think of anything to say. Except, bloody hell, is he flexible or what?"

A giggle burst out of my lips. "Oh my God. Yes, that's unnatural, right?"

It felt good to laugh. To both acknowledge the discomfort and the sheer corniness and continue to make jokes.

"I didn't know this was the porn Ferris wheel."

"Honestly, they undersold this event. I would have come for the porn Ferris wheel alone."

I snorted.

"Was that a snort?"

More heat crept up my neck. "No. I did not just snort, I swear." But the more I laughed, the more snorts came out of me. "Oh my God, this is the strangest date I've ever been on."

"And just so we're clear, I think you're smart and you're snorts are cute. Also, I don't need the porn. I was plenty turned on from the moment you opened the door. It's just that the porn is making it impossible to think about anything else."

On the screen, the man was kissing the woman's neck. His hands covered her breasts, his thumbs rubbing her nipples.

I squeezed my thighs together.

Why was this happening to me?

Because you need to live a little. You can't go anywhere for twenty minutes. Your team doesn't arrive for thirty. Have some fun.

"I'll say it again. This is the most bizarre date I've ever been on."

"I know, but I'm just going to do what I've been thinking about doing all night anyway." His hand slid up my thigh, and involuntarily, my thighs parted, granting him the access I desperately wanted him to have.

"I'm not sure this is the best idea."

"You tell me to stop, and I will."

I knew the right thing was to tell him to stop. To try and get some semblance of control back over this situation, this relationship, and my feelings for him, but I didn't want control for once in my life. Control was safe, and I knew what to do with control. But with Marcus, I felt like I was hurtling through the sky with no parachute but somehow confident that he would catch me in the end, which was ridiculous.

There's no one there to catch you.

I'd had enough shit in my life to know that. But I wanted to believe it could be true.

Here we were, with Marcus's hand on my thigh and my core pulsing with need, and all I wanted him to do was slide his hand up higher and feel how wet I was. My gaze flickered to his lips.

His groan was so low it was almost a growl. "Lyra, you are killing me right now. Tell me what you want. Tell me and I'll do it, anything you ask."

"Kiss me."

Because when he kissed me, I couldn't think of anything else. I couldn't think of all the reasons why I shouldn't be with him, why it was safer to stay away from him. I couldn't think of what the right thing to do was when I was with him and he had his tongue in my mouth and his hands on my hips, and he was grinding against me and making me feel like a real person.

Like I was allowed to live, allowed to breathe for once.

I loved everything about that feeling. It was addiction personified. I loved it that he *saw* me. Even if just in glimpses. I wanted him to see all of me.

I wanted to capture that feeling and bottle it. Never let it go.

We had twenty minutes on this Ferris wheel. Twenty minutes where I could just be Lyra and he could just be Marcus. I was going to enjoy every second of it.

I nodded to let him know this was what I wanted, his hands on me, his tongue licking into my mouth, teasing my tongue into playing. Marcus Black made me feel things. He brought to the surface all those emotions that I kept locked up so tightly. He had the key, and he knew how to use it. And for once, that didn't terrify me.

His kiss was surprisingly soft. First a whisper, then a caress, then a slow seductive slide. His tongue licked into my mouth, caressing, teasing, cajoling. His hand slid into my hair, twisting into my curls, and I felt both possessed and cherished. And neither one of those feelings were what I was accustomed to. As we kissed, my hips lifted slightly.

"Tell me what you need, Lyra."

"I need you to touch me."

"Bloody brilliant."

He went back to kissing me, but he didn't move his hand, so I raised my hips to encourage him. Which only made him chuckle as he whispered, "Stop being so impatient. I'll get there."

Oh, I had no doubt. But first, he was going to take his time and kiss me like we had all the time in the world.

He whispered against my lips. "That's it, love, open your thighs wider for me."

I dragged in a shuddering breath. All I could do was nod, because words would have led to begging.

His hand slid up my thigh, and his knuckles gently brushed over my sex. When he made contact, he dragged his lips from mine and kissed along my jaw as he said, "I've been dying to know what you felt like. It's like you've taken over my mind. There was a time when I was able to do other things, to focus on other things, but you've made that impossible."

He was close. So close. *Just a little higher.*

His knuckles grazed over my sex again, and I could hear him swallow audibly. "Oh fuck, Lyra."

"Marcus, please. Please, just touch me."

"Oh my God, you are so wet."

One of his long fingers hooked under the elastic of my panties, stroked over my clit, and sank deep. Both of us groaned. I clutched onto his shoulders and moaned, "Marcus, oh God."

"I know. I know. I'm barely even touching you, and I'm so ready to bloody blow."

Ever so gently, he made love to me with his hand. His finger sliding in and out as his thumb gave me butterfly kisses over my clit. When the pace picked up, he dragged his lips back to mine, his tongue mimicking the actions of his fingers, fucking my mouth and making me crazy. The tension coiling inside me was ready to blow.

His finger slid and retreated, slid and retreated, his thumb casting its own spell over me, drugging me slowly with his strokes and his words. Mostly hushed murmurs of *need, want, God, Lyra.*

As I gripped his shoulders, I could feel the quaking need snaking over my body. That tightly coiled tension I held inside me at all times breaking apart.

Marcus pulled back, touching his forehead to mine, his gaze locking, never letting me go. "Let me see it, Lyra. I want to watch you be free."

And then I let him see. A massive shudder wracked my body. With a muffled scream into his neck, my body tightened and convulsed around his fingers as he buried them deep within me.

I was in trouble. Marcus Black was dangerous to me, because instead of thinking ahead to my mission and my partners, people depending on me, I wanted to be on this Ferris wheel with Marcus Black forever.

I wasn't thinking about logistics or identifying the target. No, I was only thinking about Marcus and how to get more of what he just gave me. Something told me that I would be safe with him, that if at any point I wanted to be free, he would give me the freedom I needed.

I'd always thought Tyler had broken me. But I could see it clearly now; Marcus Black would be the one to destroy me.

Suddenly, sitting there on the Ferris wheel wrapped in Marcus's arms, both of us panting and breathing hard, I could hear Addie's voice in my comm unit.

"It's showtime. Switch to channel A."

I tapped my earring to change the comm channel and then tapped it twice more to let everyone know that I was on and listening but couldn't speak.

Tyler's voice came on next. "We have a sighting on Mads McLean. He's with a woman. Not sure who it is, but she's blond, tall, and has a scar on her left cheek."

And then it was Kira's voice in my ear. From her vantage point she could see them. "He handed something to the woman. He's doubling back and leaving."

I tried to keep my face neutral until I knew what to do. I waited for Tyler to come on with the command.

When he came back on, it wasn't good news. "The woman is Sasha White. She's a member of Victus, and she's been given her card for the private auction." That was when all hell broke loose. "Lyra, you're up. Get that card."

The Ferris wheel car came down to a stop, and Marcus helped me out. Desperate for an excuse, I asked him, "Do you know where the bathroom is?"

He frowned as he glanced around. "I think there is one over there."

He was pointing in the wrong direction. "Oh, okay, let's go."

Then I asked the ride attendant, "Is the bathroom over there the nearest one?"

She shook her head and pointed the other way. "No, there's one just right there."

I turned around in the direction I needed to go. "Okay, thanks." I turned to Marcus. "Do you want to wait for me here?"

Marcus frowned. "Uh, sure, okay. I'll wait for you."

I tried to give him my brightest smile. "I'll be right back. Don't you move. After this, I want funnel cake and a latte."

He nodded and then pushed me lightly in the direction of the comfort room. "Go, I'll be right here. Funnel cake, latte, and more rides after you get back."

I gave him a cheery smile. "You're on. I won't be long."

I prayed I was right.

I'd been on the lookout for Mads and waiting for a status update while we were on the Ferris wheel.

When I hadn't been occupied with Lyra.

This is a dangerous game you're playing.

I knew the game was dangerous, but I couldn't stay away from her. Not now that I knew what it could be like with us.

I wanted more. More of her, more time, but I'd never, *ever* once come close to blowing a mission.

Everything was going to shit in my comm unit. I could hear everything going wrong but couldn't respond until Lyra excused herself to the ladies' room.

"What the fuck is going on?"

When he responded, Rhodes sounded like he was running. "Stannis is a no-show. I repeat he's a no-show. Mads had a private auction meeting with someone else. A woman. He handed her something and then took off. I repeat, Mads has left the premises."

"Fuck. Do we know who she was?"

Becker's voice was clear and direct. "I'm running the facial recognition software now. It'll still take a second. But we have bigger problems."

My heart hammered as I searched the crowd for Lyra. "What do you mean?"

"We have confirmed agents from The Firm onsite. Sniper on the roof. They are likely also trying to grab Mads and Stannis."

"What's the call? What are we doing?" I scanned the crowd, looking for Lyra. She'd been gone just a little too long.

Rhodes was silent for a moment. "Instructions are to return to headquarters. If Mads is in the wind and Stannis is a no-show, we need to regroup. We are not to engage with Firm agents."

The hell we wouldn't.

It was almost as if Rhodes could hear me disobeying a direct order. His voice was very clear and suddenly very British. "Let it go, Marcus. Follow the mission command."

I didn't want to listen to reason. Didn't want to follow orders. The only thing that kept me from doing something stupid was worrying about Lyra. I glanced around, looking for any potential Firm agents. If they started shooting at someone they thought was a target, she could get caught in the crossfire, and they wouldn't care who died.

I had the simplest egress route. Just go out the way I'd come in. My only job tonight had been to tag Mads and Stannis. But things hadn't gone that way. I kept wondering what would have happened if I'd hadn't had my fingers inside of Lyra. Would I have seen them?

Maybe. But the point was that the meet had started earlier than it was supposed to and hadn't gone as planned if Stannis was a no-show. Where the fuck was Mads McLean going?

Rhodes was right. We needed to regroup and figure out

what the fuck went wrong. But first, I had to get Lyra to safety and then walk through what in the world had happened tonight with my team. I started to get nervous about Lyra when it had been ten minutes since she'd walked away. And we still didn't have any confirmation on how many Firm agents there were.

When I went after her, I couldn't believe what the hell I was seeing.

~

Lyra

I turned my back on Marcus, trying to stroll as nonchalantly as I could while also hustling. Addie's voice came in clear. "Yup, Lyra, she's up ahead, about fifty meters."

My voice was croaky as I said, "On it."

Jesus, what had made me think this was a good idea?

Get your shit together. Do this. Get the card from Sasha White, find out what happened to Prochenko and where Mads McLean went, and then maybe you can go out with Marcus for real.

I hoped I could fucking go out with Marcus for real, because I really did like him.

I looked in the women's restroom, but I didn't see anyone. What had gone wrong and why were they meeting early? "Are you sure she's here?"

Addie said, "No, she's in the alley behind the bathroom."

I ran out to the darkened alley and found it to be a dead end.

What was I missing? I looked for a door that led into some other building, but I couldn't see one. Maybe it was further down. "Ad—"

I never even heard the metal pipe until it sliced through

the air with a whoosh. I jumped out of the way just in time. Sasha had overshot her mark. Before she could even whirl around to swing at me again, I kicked her in the kidney. With a grunt, she dropped the pipe, and it made a clanging sound.

"We don't have to do this. I just want a little information."

"You won't get it out of me," she spat as she came at me again. This time, she tried to grab me around the midsection to pick me up.

She could have too, since she had three inches and several pounds on me. But as she wrapped her arms around me, I brought down my elbow and tackled her back. She grunted, but she didn't release me. A couple more well-placed elbows, and her hold finally loosened. As soon as it did, I reached my arms out wide and then clapped my palms hard over her ears.

She swung at me again, and I blocked it with my left arm, bringing my elbow in and then dragging it up as far as I could, right next to my head to block her. I delivered a punch, which she blocked easily.

It was then that I heard footsteps. "Lyra?"

At that single moment of distraction, my attention was split.

I could hear it, the twang of metal, and I called out to him to keep him from coming toward danger. "Marcus, no, I—" I blocked the knife, hit her again, and then tried to turn around to stop him from entering the alley.

But he headed toward me surprisingly fast as he yelled, "Lyra, what in the—"

I never even saw her fist coming. Sasha got me right in the jaw. I instantly fell to the ground, dizzy. It made my eyes sting and my jaws clang together.

Oh fuck, that was going to bruise.

"Oh my God, Lyra."

Marcus. I had to think of something fast. I yelled at Sasha, "For the last time, I have no intention of ever having anything to do with your boyfriend. He's all yours."

When she saw Marcus, I sensed momentary indecision on her face. She probably contemplated whether to strike me again with him added to the equation or go. And for some reason, she opted to make a run for it.

Fuck. I tapped my comm and whispered, "Target is in the wind. I repeat, target is in the wind."

In all the commotion and the noisiness of the fair rides, I didn't think Marcus heard me.

He was too focused on coming for me as I lay on the ground.

In my earpiece, I could hear Addie, Tyler, and Roz as the pandemonium set in and they went after Sasha.

They knew my location. Hopefully, they could fucking get her. I'd failed. After all that, I'd *failed*.

Marcus kneeled down next to me. "Jesus Christ, what in the world is going on?"

I groaned as I held my jaw. "Oh God, that really hurt."

"Who was that?"

"Um, new girlfriend of my ex. Tyler. You met him. A bit of a dick."

His eyes went wide. "What?"

"She saw me by the bathroom. When I was coming out, she cornered me. You know, a stay-away-from-my-man kind of thing."

He frowned. "That's ridiculous."

"I know, right?" Ugh, I really needed to get better with my lies.

Luckily, in the dark he couldn't really see me that well.

"Jesus, do you want to call the police?"

"No, I just... I need ice."

"Yup, coming right up. How come every time we go out something wild happens?"

"I swear to God, it's not me."

He laughed. "Jesus, we need to get you some basic self-defense class or something."

"Yeah, that's something to think about for sure."

Thirty minutes later, we were in Marcus's apartment. Me with an icepack on my face, him with heat lamps on, checking me all over to make sure that I didn't have any other injuries.

My ribs were tender, so I really hoped to God he wouldn't press too hard on them. "Did she hit you anywhere else?"

"Well, she tried to hit me with a pole, but I ducked away, and then I dropped and hurt myself a little."

"God, Lyra, I mean it. We really need to get you in some basic self-defense course."

"What, now you're an expert on self-defense?"

"No, not exactly, but I know when someone's going to get hurt one day. And you are that woman."

Not if I could help it.

12

MARCUS

For fuck's sake, it was like danger followed Lyra around. I helped her settle the icepack gently over her cheekbone, and I frowned as she winced.

Not your circus, not your monkeys.

I wanted them to be my monkeys. She'd nearly gotten herself in trouble.

"Why don't you tell me her name?"

Lyra's brows rose. "Why?"

Why was she so stubborn about this? "So I can file a police report. She tried to assault you." When she shook her head vehemently, I added, "Okay, then tell me the surname of your ex. I can look him up. Maybe reach out to him and let him know his girlfriend is crazy."

"Oh no you don't. I'll deal with this."

I laughed. "Why won't you let me help you with this?"

"I'm fine. Honestly. She didn't hit that hard."

I laughed at that. "Sweetheart, I don't think you can see your jaw right now." I lifted the icepack away from her face.

"It's going to be a big bruise. It's going to match the one under your eye."

"I can see it in your face. You think something is happening to me. Honestly, nothing is happening. I am just clumsy, and you saw it today."

"Yeah, I saw it. Obviously, I'm just really worried."

She sighed and reached up to touch my face. "Do you realize no one has worried about me this much in years? Not since my parents died."

It had been a long time since I was aware of my heart, but right now it wanted to do anything and everything to make Lyra feel better.

"Well, maybe someone should."

"I've learned to be independent."

"It's not all or nothing, Lyra. I reckon your ex did a number on you. And we don't have to talk about it yet, but one day you'll open up to me about him. In the meantime, I want Tyler's surname. I would like to have a conversation with him about his girlfriend, as well as whatever the hell he did to you that makes you keep your guard up so high."

"Well, we don't always get what we want, do we? I'll deal with it. I don't want you involved because that sends the message that I can't deal with things on my own and need some hero to swoop in and take care of me."

I gritted my teeth. I wanted to fix this for her. And by fix, I meant making that asshole ex-boyfriend of hers pay for everything he'd ever done to her and then getting his current girlfriend to come do his dirty work.

You're not thinking clearly. If she doesn't want you to fix it, don't fix it.

The thing was, she clearly needed someone to take care of her.

"Okay, if you won't let me talk to him and you won't call the police, then at least let me teach you some self-defense moves."

She lifted a brow. "Well, first of all, I don't think I need self-defense moves. Secondly, *you're* going to teach me self-defense?"

I nodded slowly, wondering how much I could tell her and why in the world she sounded incredulous. "Yeah, I did Krav Maga for years."

She blinked in surprise. "Oh. I didn't know that."

I shrugged. "It was years ago. But I still remember the basics enough so that you can defend yourself and never leave yourself open."

She ran a hand through her hair and looked a little doubtful.

"Let me do this. It'll make me feel better."

She looked like she was going to argue some more, but then she didn't. "Fine. If you insist."

"Good, maybe tomorrow we'll get started, okay?"

"Where have you been hiding, Marcus Black?"

"You keep asking that. I've been right here."

"And what, I just didn't notice you before?"

"That must be it."

"Believe me, I'm pretty sure I would have noticed."

"Sometimes we don't see things that are right in front of our eyes."

"If you say so."

I placed a thumb over her bruised cheek, and she frowned. "You've got that look on your face again. The one that says you want to ride in on your white horse and save me or something."

"Yeah, well, I want to save you, but I don't think you'll

let me."

"How about we pretend I don't need saving? Or even better, let's pretend I'm saving you."

"I can't help it. There's something about you that makes me want to protect you."

She pulled back a little. "And if I told you I don't need protecting?"

My fingers dusted over her cheek again. I didn't dare touch her jaw because I didn't want to hurt her. "I think we all need protecting sometimes," I said with a wink.

She swallowed and then tilted her chin up. "Marcus?"

"Yeah?"

"Maybe instead of worrying about me, you could kiss me again." Her tongue peeked out to moisten her lips a little.

The roar of rushing blood in my ears made it difficult to think clearly. "Lyra, you're making this impossible."

"I know. Kiss me anyway."

"I want to be the good guy."

She shook her head. "Right now, I don't want a good guy."

So I leaned down and showed her just what a bad boy I could be.

MARCUS

The scent of coconut and lime wrapped around me. Lyra tasted sweet with a little chaser of something spicier. She parted her lips with a gasp, and I deepened the kiss, licking into her mouth. I wanted more.

I knew this was a bad idea. I knew I wasn't good for her and that if I did this, I wouldn't want to let her go. And the truth of it was that at some point I might have to, because being with me might be dangerous for her.

Like a fool, I didn't stop though. I just tortured myself by pulling her tighter against me, my hand smoothing over her back and dragging her against me, fitting her body to mine and making sure she could feel every inch of how much I craved her.

I angled my head with a groan, dipping my knees slightly as I lifted her so that our bodies fit together and I could capture her mouth better. She was so small in comparison to me, but she was strong. I could feel the muscles in her thighs as they gripped my waist. There was nothing delicate or dainty about her, and I loved it.

My tongue stroked over hers, darting, and playing, and sliding. She kept making these sexy little mewling sounds at the back of her throat like she was bloody well egging me on. Daring me to take more and deliberately trying to drive me mad.

My hands slid into her hair, enjoying the soft, bouncy feel of her curls in my grip. Desperate for her, I tugged just a little and she gasped, lifting her face to mine. When our eyes locked, her lips curved up into a secretive smile. And I knew it then... Lyra Wilkinson was going to kill me.

Her smile was luminescent and immediately had all the blood rushing to my cock. There would be no 'just this one time.' There would be no casual fling with her. The way I responded to her, my blood pumping through my veins, burning me up as lava chased desire, I knew she was going to end me. And right about then, my dick didn't care.

Our kiss was a clash of tongues and teeth and lips, and I squeezed her ass as I positioned her the way I wanted her. Lyra rolled her hips against mine, sliding her sweet heat over my cock, and the next thing I knew I was blindly moving. I needed some place flat. Any flat surface would do.

My first option, obviously, was the bedroom. But I hadn't expected this. I'd thought I'd take her home to her place, and I wasn't sure exactly what was lying around my bedroom so taking her there might be a mistake. So, next best thing? The balcony. The daybed out there was plenty big enough, and besides, this wasn't going to get that far. This was just a kiss.

Sure, keep telling yourself that.

Lyra kept working her hips against mine as we kissed, my tongue sliding into her mouth, orally fucking her like I was so desperate to do with my cock.

Fuck. Me.

The night was warm, the air balmy, when I stepped out onto the balcony. I sat down on the daybed, dragging her to face me and fitting her perfectly so she could brace herself and use me if she wanted.

Once we were settled, we fought for dominance. Lyra's inner thighs squeezed my hips as she rolled up and down over the length of my dick and made me see stars.

After the taste of her on the Ferris wheel earlier, feeling her sweet, slick heat, my hands were shaking as I slid one up under her skirt, enjoying the silken feel of her firm thighs.

My hands pushed up the fabric as they teased her skin. When I reached the edge of her panties, I held my breath, giving her time to stop me.

She didn't.

When my thumb slipped under the elastic she gasped. "Marcus."

"Do you want me to stop?"

She pulled back, her dark gaze on mine. "No. Please, no."

I already knew how wet she'd be, the sweet slickness I

would find. But still, I wanted so much more. I wanted to make this so good for her.

"Just—please—Marcus—touch me."

"Oh trust me. I am."

Slowly I traced my thumb over her slick flesh until I reached that sweet button and pressed ever so lightly. Lyra threw her head back, groaning. I took full advantage then. With one hand under her, I embraced her back and guided her just where I wanted, leaning forward and wrapping my mouth over her nipple through the thin cotton of her top and the outlines of the lacy bra that had been teasing me all night.

Lyra's hands dug into my hair, holding me close to her as she rocked her hips even more against my thumb. It wasn't enough. I needed to see her too. I knew I could make her come just like this, but I needed more.

With a frustrated growl, I pulled my hand from her panties and ripped my lips off her nipple. She groaned in frustration, trying to pull me back. Her insistence made me chuckle. "Oh don't worry, I'm coming back."

But first, she needed to be wearing a lot less clothing. I reached for the hem of her T-shirt, gently easing it up, and she urged me along by raising her arms, helping me to get it off.

When she was bare to me, I saw that her bra was this mint green, lace, half-cup situation that barely covered her tits. A hint of dusky cinnamon nipple peeked out, taunting me, and I muttered a curse. "Bloody hell, God is a woman, and she's a fucking tease."

Lyra's eyes had been searching mine, but my low, husky words seemed to make her smile. I wasn't really paying attention to her smile at that moment, even though I knew how brilliant it was. I couldn't quite tear my eyes off the prize. "You are so fucking gorgeous."

She reached behind herself, unclasping her bra and letting it fall off of her shoulders.

I stared. That was the only way it could be explained. All higher brain functioning was lost, all blood having vacated to the organ that needed it the most. My dick. High and firm, peaked with cinnamon-tipped nipples, her tits were my new obsession.

My hands slid up her ribcage until I palmed both breasts, squeezing gently until she moaned as I murmured, "Your skin is so fucking sensational." Or at least I think I said something to that effect. I was too distracted. My thumbs rolled over her nipples as I watched her reaction closely, ferreting out what she liked and what she didn't like.

And because I couldn't help myself, I leaned forward again, this time wrapping my lips around her sweet flesh. Then I groaned, the sound low and guttural and completely primal. It felt like someone had struck my dick with lightning.

"Oh my God, Marcus."

A harsh laugh tore out of my chest.

"Okay, love," I murmured. "I'll keep going."

I wanted to leave no stone unturned, no part of her skin unexplored. I worshipped both breasts, from the pebbled peaks to the sensitive full curve underneath, and I took my time. Used my tongue, teasing those pretty tips, occasionally scraping them with my teeth. Lyra started to thrash, and I held her steady. Her hands left my hair, and she began tugging at my shirt.

I dragged it up my back to oblige but then realized I was going to have to let go of her nipple to get the damn thing off.

With a frustrated growl, I released her, making a smacking sound.

As soon as my shirt was off, her hands began rolling over my muscles, my shoulders, my pecs, all the while riding over the one organ she wanted most. "Lyra, you're going to have to stop grinding on me, or I'm going to blow inside my jeans. I really don't want that, and I think you're not going to enjoy that either."

"I want to see you lose control."

"Are you kidding me? I'm riding the edge with you right now." How could she not see how badly I was shaking? How could she not understand how desperate I was?

"Marcus, please."

She wanted to see me lose control. She wanted me to let go. "Lyra—"

Her hands caressed my face. "Just let go. You're safe with me."

How could she have known how desperately I needed those gentle words? I met her gaze to understand the truth of what she was saying to me.

And for the first time in three years, I loosened the reins of my control.

～

Lyra

It was almost as if Marcus had been waiting for permission to lose control. He changed our positions so that he was laying over me but shifted most of his weight to the side so he wouldn't crush me. Then he let out a whoosh of air.

The man who had been so gentle and delicate and careful with me now wasted no time. He shoved a hand in my hair, tugging my head back while gently forcing me to arch my back and put my breasts on display for him.

With a feral growl, he wrapped his lips around one and sucked. *Hard.* The motion sent shockwaves of need and pinpricks of aching desire straight to my sex. Before, his lips had been teasing, but this time he meant business. As I lay under him, squirming, he laid loving siege to both breasts, licking them, sucking them, teasing them with his teeth, making me squirm and beg.

"Oh my God, Marcus." My hips rose with the need to be touched. "Please. I just need—"

Against my breasts, he mumbled, "Oh, I know what you need."

Those six words had my panties completely soaked. He knew, all right. With his mouth busy, his one free hand slid down my torso and back to the edge of my panties, dipping his fingers in and finding the slick button he was more than a little acquainted with now.

My hips bucked. As he sucked on my nipples, he slid two fingers deep inside me, and I gasped. "Holy shit."

If I didn't know better, I would swear the man chuckled. But I was too preoccupied with the delicious things his fingers were doing to me as his thumb circled my clit and his mouth sucked on me and his hand gently fisted in my hair. Marcus Black meant business.

I could feel it coming, the impending orgasm, the electricity crackling up my spine and making me start to shake. Marcus just kept up the onslaught, driving me to the outcome with a quick efficiency that was terrifying. He absolutely knew what he was doing. And he knew how to get there.

He released me abruptly, and my nipples ached in the cool air.

With quick, deliberate movements, Marcus unzipped my skirt and pulled it down along with my panties. His kisses down my body were lingering, teasing, until he reached my clit.

All I heard was a muttered curse from him before he pulled his fingers from me and replaced them with his mouth. I couldn't really form coherent thought after that.

He showed the same kind of expertise with long laps of his tongue, teasing around my clit but never quite giving me what I wanted.

My legs started to shake and thrash on the daybed. "Please, I'm begging you, Marcus. Please." What was that song? I wasn't too proud to beg. Nope. I would beg all day if it meant Marcus would give me another orgasm. In that moment, I didn't care how I got it, but I really, *really* wanted to make love to him.

He lifted his head and gave me the devil's own smile. "This is what happens when I lose control, Lyra. I do the thing that I have been dreaming about doing since I first saw you. I've been desperate to know how you taste."

"Can I taste you too?"

His icy blue eyes had gone so dark that they were nearly black. His tongue licked over his bottom lip. "Fuck yes. But first I need to be inside you, or I might actually die."

I didn't need any convincing. I sat up, and with shaking fingers, I helped him with his belt and tried to help push down his jeans. But it was more of a comedy of errors, so finally he just did the honors. As soon as they were off, he chucked them over his shoulder, but not before grabbing his wallet and a condom.

He tossed the wallet on the table he had next to the daybed and then turned back to me. My gaze immediately landed below his waist, and my mouth fell open. "Jesus, Lord. Wow. You are seriously…"

The grin he gave me was wickedly playful. And I realized it wasn't often he grinned like that in a sort of carefree, swagger kind of way. When he hooked his thumbs in his boxers and took them down, my mouth went dry. He was *huge*.

Sure, maybe my horniness was making me exaggerate, but I didn't think so. Marcus Black was like my birthday and Christmas rolled into one.

He sheathed himself quickly before climbing back into the daybed and settling between my thighs. "You okay?" he asked as he rubbed his nose on the column of my neck, making me shiver.

"You recognize that you're huge, right?"

There was that grin again. All swagger and big-dick energy. "Something tells me we're going to fit just right."

Marcus took his time revving my engines back up, albeit easily. He started with slow kisses, the ones intended to drug me into a stupor with his skill, and then he began kissing my breasts again. Note to self: Marcus Black was a boob man. And with every lick and nibble and caress, I was raising my hips, begging him to sink inside me.

When his dick was notched against my slippery wet sex, he dropped his forehead to mine. His voice was a raspy whisper when he spoke. "We can go slow if—"

But I didn't let him finish. Instead I lifted my hips, taking him to the hilt. We both froze.

"Fuck, Lyra."

"Oh my God."

He lifted his head immediately. "Too much?"

What the hell was he talking about? This was… wow.

"Stop talking so much."

On his retreat, he chuckled low. "Yes, love. Whatever you say, love."

When he drove forward again, I gasped. Holy hell. This was what I'd been missing out on all this time?

His face was a mask of grim determination and concentration. His slow slide and retreat, slide and retreat, was driving me insane. I just wanted to—

The shaking started in my toes and traveled up my body like a shock wave. When it hit my spine, I was done for.

I squeezed my eyes shut, wanting to ride out the wave of intense pleasure as it took over all my nerve endings, but Marcus's demand was sharp. "Look at me, Lyra. I want you to watch me lose control. All because of you."

As waves of pleasure sent me cascading in bliss, the edges of my vision grew bleary as my body vibrated with ecstasy. Marcus scooped his hands under my ass, bracing me in position, as he continued to love me with a relentless slide and retreat as he watched me.

"C'mon Lyra, give me one more. One more and I'll lose control. I promise."

"Oh God, I don't know if I can" I whispered on a pant.

Marcus dipped his head, watching where we were joined. "Something tells me you can." He changed his hand position, holding my ass with only one hand, the other reaching around me so he could slide his thumb over my clit.

And sure enough, I broke again on a muffled scream, my whole body convulsing and quaking. With his thumb still on my clit, his voice was gravel when he said, "Fuuuuck, why is this so goddamn good?"

And then he chased me into oblivion as his release shook his body.

13

MARCUS

I stared at Michael. "This is the second or third mission in the last two weeks where The Firm has also been there. Do you want to tell me what the fuck is going on?"

Michael was a master of not showing emotion, as if his agents failing was an occurrence that he would accept. Except he and I both knew better. He didn't tolerate failure. And someone was going to be held responsible for what happened at the Bacchanal.

It was no one else's fault but mine. If I had been watching, I'd have seen Mads. Instead, I'd been watching Lyra. I needed to keep everyone safe. For the integrity of my team and the safety of Lyra, I needed to mitigate this risk. "How did we not know Stannis wasn't going to show up? What happened to him? It's not like he would get cold feet."

Michael sat back. "Unless he made his arrangement at another time. Or it's entirely possible they got spooked for some reason. Maybe they changed the time that they plan to meet. It might still be on. So we have to figure out a way into that mission."

I ran my hands through my hair. "I was the problem, sir. I didn't see Mads."

Michael looked bored. "My understanding was that the meet happened early. Becker caught him in her scope by accident."

"Still, sir, I should have been more vigilant. My team depends on me."

"That they do. Is there something in particular that you're trying to say? Because right now I see you trying to accept accountability for something we couldn't have known. We don't have all the pieces, and we're missing something. So let's backtrack, find out the last place we saw Stannis, and figure out where he went from there. And let's get someone to wrangle us an invitation to that very private party that Mads is having. I don't care what we have to do to get that weapon."

"But sir, I worry that we won't have enough details. We're flying blind."

Michael rubbed his jaw. "I have a source. You know they're not always the most trustworthy, but I think I'll get the honest truth out of him for this. I'll find out. And Marcus?"

"Yes, Michael?"

"This isn't like the Simone situation. We don't know for certain if The Firm is involved."

Michael might not believe The Firm was involved in all this, but I certainly wasn't accepting that answer. I walked out of his office even more confident in the truth. The Firm, a rival agency, had killed my fiancée, and someone from my side was feeding them intel about missions. It was the only explanation for why they'd shown up at so many of our jobs lately. They had to have an inside track, which meant I might not be able to trust my own people.

Lyra

I learned long ago not to trust Roz's calm voice. It usually meant that there was rage simmering somewhere inside. And you were better off getting the rage over with right away. Because simmering rage, that shit was going to go nuclear.

"Explain to me what happened."

It didn't matter how many times I had gone over this; she was going to make me repeat it and repeat it until she was either satisfied or I was blue in the face and dead. Whichever came faster. "I've told you. Comms came on. Addie let me know locations. I was on the Ferris wheel on watch. I could see everything. As Mads approached, there was a woman waiting. To most it would have looked like a date or something. They hugged and kissed. And then he handed her something silver, small. Like a credit card. Kira clocked the exchange and made the note. And then, once we found out who she was, I chased her down."

She nodded slowly, as if all that sounded correct, but something was still very, very wrong. "But explain to me again how you lost this fight."

So it was going to be that kind of a day. Nothing was going to satisfy her. "I said I'm sorry. But haven't you noticed? We've had a series of failures lately."

"Yes, and the common denominator seems to be you."

"I've been working missions to the best of my ability. Having Tyler here isn't exactly easy."

It was a good thing I had long since given up on finding

real understanding with her. "Don't give me excuses. I want answers. And why the fuck was Exodus there?"

I stared at her. "We have a confirmed sighting?"

"We do. After all, Kira wasn't the only sniper on the roof. I want to know why Exodus agents are all over my people."

What the hell? "I don't know. I didn't even see them. I was on the Ferris wheel to do my job. Remember?"

"What is it your boyfriend does again?"

"Marcus? He's a video game designer."

"And he was with you the entire time? I just want to make sure that any mistakes of yours aren't a reflection of him. Because he will be removed from your life if necessary."

I wasn't backing down though. She used that tactic on me a lot when I was still in college. Threatening to take away my favorite outfit, or threatening not to give me missions because I had failed a class. She didn't understand that her coming down on me like that just made me work harder. I was my own worst critic. "You can count on me. I will get the job done."

"No more mistakes Lyra. None of us can afford anymore."

Maybe I hadn't thought through this whole *teach Lyra a few things* idea. The following afternoon, we were in the gym that was next to our flat, and she was wearing these leggings that should be illegal.

They were vermillion red that seemed to make her brown skin glow, and she'd paired them with a cut off T-shirt that kept showing me oh-so-intriguing glimpses of her midriff.

My concentration was nonexistent. All my energy was directed to making my eyeballs stay on her face and not stray to her tits or her midriff. Or, fuck me to Soho and back, that arse I was itching to take a bite of.

"Like this?" she asked.

I gently encapsulated Lyra's hand with my own, showing her how to tighten her fist and where to place her thumb for maximum impact. Her skin was so damn soft. And Christ, she smelled good.

My dick was already having a hard time remembering that this session we were having was for practical purposes. To protect her. To keep her safe.

You mean when you can't. Or even better, when you're the cause of danger.

This sizzling spark of connection between us was dangerous. I hadn't even realized I was searching for something like this.

It was foolhardy.

But what if it wasn't? What if this was what Rhodes and Curtis had been talking about? Having someone to come home to, someone I could care about.

Curtis had once told me it was policy because when Aidan Saint-James and Orion McClintock founded the original agency, they had seen what the isolation could do to their agents. They were efficient, but they only had a shell of a life. The moment they gave them something to care about, they became more stable and lasted longer in the job.

So our agents were encouraged to have relationships. But obviously, operators couldn't tell their partners anything about what they really did, so there was still a bit of distance there. Exodus never wanted an agent who would choose loyalty to their partner over loyalty to their agency.

And you might care a little too much about Lyra. You would just about give up every dime you have just to see her smile.

She grinned up at me. "Like this?"

I nodded slowly, my eyes focusing on her lips. When she pulled the bottom of her lip with her perfectly straight white teeth, I groaned. "Lyra, you're trying to distract me."

"I am not. I'm here to learn. I am making a fist. Look at me with my fist."

"Okay, let's try a couple of combinations with the pads. Remember what I showed you about making sure you keep your guard up? When you punch, you want to tuck your head just a little bit into your neck, kind of like a turtle. You don't want to give anyone an easy target, yeah? And keep your arm locked in. You don't want to swing wide because you're losing the power of your force in that arc. You got me?"

"Um, okay. Tight fist, tuck my neck, hands up. Sure, got it."

I loved her determined face. The furrow of her brow, the slight bite of her cheek that she always did, my little warrior. She wasn't terrible either. She just needed time and work.

And let me guess, you volunteer all the time to put in the work with her?

I just wanted her to be able to take care of herself. I would never get the image of her getting hit out of my head. I hated it. She delivered some blows to the bag, still swinging a little too wildly. "Put your hips into it, and remember what I said, lock your arms. Keep them straight."

More lip biting. More nodding. More combinations.

When I started to notice that she had sweat on her brow, I gave her a break.

"It's good to get a workout in. Kickboxing is fun, but I guess not that applicable to a real-world fight. It's not like I'm doing the stuff you see in MMA or anything."

I helped her take off the gloves. "Hey, it's okay. Most people aren't. Most sane people anyway."

"How come you know so much about self-defense? I know you said that you did Krav Maga, right?"

"Yeah. And I also did a lot of jujitsu when I was younger."

"Wow, all these things I didn't know about you."

"Yeah, well, lots to learn, isn't there?"

She tossed the towel over her shoulder after she dabbed her eyebrows. "So how does an adorable computer geek come to learn jujitsu and Krav Maga?"

I laughed. "Remember, I said I have brothers, right?"

"Yes, but that doesn't... I mean, I'm sure boys fight, but to take it so far as to need to learn martial arts?"

The giant floor-to-ceiling windows of the gym let in so much light. The sunlight was dancing in her hair, adding streaks of brown, gold, and auburn to her curls.

"My older brother, Liam, is military, British SAS, and let's just say kids who love computers and programming aren't exactly the popular kids."

She winced. "Right. I could see that."

"So, anyway, I had my arse kicked. A lot."

"Oh no."

"Eventually, I got a lot bigger. But I also got into gaming hard core. Wanted to build my own games. So I started taking jujitsu and Krav Maga so I could have a good enough understanding of the moves to design games."

"That's so cool. It must have come in incredibly handy."

I laughed. "Yes, handy indeed."

"Even nerdy, you must have been cute though."

I shook my head and laughed. "Uh, no. I was awkward. Gangly. For the longest time, I was small. So small."

She stared at me, brows lifted. "No way."

"Yes, way. I honestly didn't see sunlight once for three weeks on a holiday break. Mom was beside herself. I was a proper geek. I stayed inside the house on a steady diet of American snacks from the corner shop."

"What was your favorite?"

"Cheetos and Mountain Dew."

She wrinkled her nose. "Ugh, those are the worst. You know that."

"I'm sorry, but Cheetos are excellent. They're the right kind of radioactive goodness that you need. Don't get me wrong. Mum made sure that I ate actual food. But the moment she wasn't looking, all the crisps I snuck didn't do anything except make my skin oily and acne prone."

She stared at me. "There isn't a hint of a scrawny, geeky kid inside you."

"Yeah, it was brutal at school. Luckily, my brothers were there, otherwise, the ass-kicking would have been much worse."

"Fuck, I'm so sorry."

"Nah, don't be sorry. Liam, he comes through for you when you need him. And he did. The kind of fighting that Liam did in the military was hugely different than what I eventually learned to do. But still, it saved my life."

"You know what? It's sort of weird for you to actually be a video game designer with that body."

"Well, I couldn't stay a gangly, awkward kid forever. I grew ten inches over the course of a couple of summers, then one big final burst, and now here I am."

She blinked. "Somehow, I don't think that's a prescription most people can follow. Eat crisps, play video games, grow ten inches over a couple of summers."

I laughed at that. "I mean I grew naturally, but the muscles, those took work. Liam eventually introduced me to this bloke at the gym he used to go to. He taught me that what I lacked in size, I could make up for with speed. And I did."

"Okay so you told me about Liam, that's your brother, right? Is he the one with the son named Evan?"

I frowned, about to correct her that it was Ella, but then I remembered my lie, so I covered. There was no letting my guard down with her.

"Ah, Evan, yeah. He's pretty stinking cute."

"I love how your whole face lights up when you're talking about him."

"I can't help it. The little sucker is adorable, you know?"

"Do you ever want a son of your own?"

I couldn't explain the sudden tightening of my chest then, the desire to answer her honestly, but I kept it together. "Yeah, you know, one day. I'm only twenty-seven. I guess I have time."

She nodded. "Yeah. One day will come soon enough, won't it?"

"Yeah, I guess."

Uncomfortable with the direction of our conversation, I turned it on her. "How about your family?"

She laughed and shook her head. "No, today it's all about you and your family and friends. Who do you hang out with? I don't think I've seen many people at your place."

"Oh, my best mate, Rhodes. I go to his place a lot. His fiancée is an excellent cook."

"Oh, that's fun. How did you guys meet?"

Fuck me. "Oh, you know, work. I was doing a game component for a company and had to work with Rhodes. He's a software developer."

"Ah, geeks unite."

"Yeah." She was going to get really suspicious if she ever saw Rhodes and I together. We looked more like what we were, stone cold killers, than the geeky types. But that was our cover. "You should meet him some time."

The words were out of my mouth before I could think about what I was saying. What the fuck was wrong with me? I was clearly losing it. Being surrounded by her scent had my brain muddled.

Separation. I needed to separate. The problem was that while my brain was giving the command, my body was not complying. Wholly non-compliant. As a matter of fact, it was leaning toward her as she was smiling up at me with those big dark eyes, staring clear into my soul, and I was convinced she would know that I was lying to her.

Then convince her, because her life depends on it.

I cleared my throat. "Ah, that's enough soul baring."

"But I like your soul bare. There's something about the way you talk about your family. It's like I can see them. It's palpable."

She wound her arms around my neck and my brain sent out the warning signals. *Danger. Danger. Too close.*

Then my heart did that tripping thing it always did around her. Christ, I could get lost in this woman. Really, really lost.

Determined to help her though, I cleared my throat. "Ready to go again?"

She took one last swig of her water and gave me a determined nod. "Yup, put me in coach."

I laughed. "What am I going to do with you?"

"You, fine sir, are going to teach me to be a badass."

Lyra

"Oh my God, you had that poor man trying to teach you how to fight?"

I winced, all the while laughing. "I know. I felt terrible. I can lie with my mouth, and even with my face, but to make my body forget muscle memory is just impossible." He had seemed to marvel at how quickly I'd picked up the punches and blocks he'd shown me.

Tyler was on our comms. "Would you two fucking focus?"

Addie and I were on standby for the surveillance team

looking for Prochenko and his contact. Since he hadn't shown up for that meet at the fair, we'd had to rely on chatter to get another bead on him. Sometimes you just got lucky.

"You know what, Tyler? Set us to B channel. If they move, we'll let you know." With that declaration, Addie disconnected the line.

I rolled my eyes. "Addie, I'm pretty sure Roz isn't going to like that."

"Frankly, I don't care what Roz likes. Saddling us with Tyler? That's cruel and unusual punishment."

"Yeah, tell me about it."

"Okay so, back to the man that you're actually interested in. Tell me the truth, who's better in bed, Tyler or Marcus?"

I laughed, even as I took the binoculars and swept for our target. "There is no competition. Hands down, it's Marcus." Because when I was with him, I didn't have to search for connection. It was there. It was evident in the way he looked at me, watched me. Made sure I was connected with him at all times. Yes, he was clearly very, very good in bed, which meant he had more practice than I wanted to even think about. But Marcus was real. It had *felt* real. And I was in more danger with him than I had ever been with Tyler.

I forced my attention on the task at hand. The house was dark. No movement, no nothing. "Is this the house? This feels wrong. It's almost too quiet. Do we have the right location?"

Addie and I switched to Channel A. "Tyler, are you sure it's 100 Crescents?"

"Yes. We've got other agents stationed there. Crescents Road, we're in the right place. Sit tight."

We shrugged and went back to watching. "Okay so, how did you manage to pretend you didn't know how to fight? You're really good at hand-to-hand combat. One of the best. I mean, Roz trained you herself. Everyone tells the new recruits the story of how you put your handler on her ass."

I winced as I remembered. "To be fair, when she said go, I didn't think of it as training. She'd said I'd have to fight for my life one day, and I didn't want to get sent home. So I *was* fighting for my life."

She shook her head, chuckling. "Only you."

I shrugged. "These things happen." I never did understand the point of doing anything for practice. If I was going to do it, I needed it to be perfect the first time. My little way of making my parents proud even though they weren't there to see me.

I rolled my lips over my teeth, trying to contain the giggle. Addie's eyes went wide.

"Oh my God, I need details about Marcus. First of all, what are we working with?" She waggled her eyebrows.

I barely stifled a giggle. "You know that moment when you reach into your date's pants and you pray, like really pray, like you call on the Holy Mother, and Buddha, and the God you haven't seen since Christmas, 2000?"

She nodded.

"My prayers were answered."

She howled and cackled with laughter. "Oh my God. Yes, thank you dick gods. Thank you for listening. I feel like we need to sacrifice a goat or something."

With a chuckle, I said, "You sound like my mother."

She gave me a soft smile before I even realized what I had said. It was in reference to my mother, which I never did.

"That is the highest compliment."

"You didn't even know her."

"No, but I know how reverently you talk about her, if you

talk about her at all, which is rarely and almost never. So if you brought her up, then that's great."

I sighed. "I know that look on your face. You're giving me that look that says you think Marcus is changing me."

"Isn't he?"

That was a good question. And by the way, how many ways had he changed me? I felt like me. I looked like me. Like I felt it deep inside. That shift. Even after Roz had gotten me into her section and I finally had family again, there was a part of me that always felt a little like... I don't know... like I was separate. Not really part of a whole. And I didn't know why I felt that way. Roz had always made me feel like I was her own. And everyone in the section had made me feel the same way too. Like I was legacy. Like they were all my family. But still, every now and again, I would get that feeling that said, this is not your family. They were my friends, and they were the family that I'd made. I just wondered what my parents would have thought of this life. Sometimes I envisioned going to their graves and telling them all about my life. How I'd grown up, who I was now, and that I saved lives and did something important with my life. But I could never go back to their graves on the off chance that somebody was following me.

A few times, I'd gone back to where I'd grown up in Massachusetts and walked through the cemetery, visited graves near theirs, but never theirs, because Lyra Adamson didn't exist anymore. Her parents had died when she was eighteen. She'd lived with her aunt for a year, who hadn't been particularly keen on taking care of her but had done so out of some sense of duty. And then, when she turned nineteen, Lyra Adamson disappeared, and Lyra Thomas, Lyra Burton, and Lyra Wilkinson were born.

"So, you let him win?"

Her question dragged me out of my reverie. "No, I let him show me how to fight. It's different. And by the way, he's had Krav Maga and jujitsu training, so it's kind of amazing really. Plus, I get to reinforce my fighting skills with his techniques."

"Yes, but his jujitsu and Krav Maga twice a week does not equate to your years of training."

"I know, I know. It's just nice to have something worthwhile to do while being in that situation, you know?"

She studied me. "Lyra, you're not falling for him, are you? Like, actually falling? Not just in the *God, it's so nice to finally bone someone who knows what to do with his dick* kind of way?"

"No, it's not that serious. I'm just enjoying it. I never get to do that."

"Well, in that case, I'm happy for you. Enjoy the ride."

I smacked her on the shoulder. "Addie!"

"What? What a wild *ride* it must be." She gave me a cheeky grin and waggled her eyebrows.

I snorted a laugh. "Oh my God, you're impossible."

"Yes, but I've never been more accurate. Look, a little friendly advice though?"

I sighed. "Let me guess, you're going to give it to me whether I want it or not?"

"Yeah, because I love you. I think this is great. Dating, meeting someone, but there is a reason why The Firm doesn't want us getting *too* close to people. You've got to find a way to keep some emotional distance. You understand that, right? I'm just worried because you seem like you're not keeping as distant as you should."

I met her gaze and saw that her blue eyes were filled with concern and worry. "I've got it, Addie, I promise. I won't lose my head."

"Famous last words."

As I turned my attention back on the quaint Spanish stone house in the corner, I wondered if she had a right to be worried. I wanted Marcus, but was I putting him in danger? If Control thought that I was getting too close to him, they'd put a stop to it, one way or the other. So I needed to be careful before I lost my heart and he lost his life all in one blow.

MARCUS

I had Lyra on the brain. I was in the office for a briefing that had temporarily pushed Stannis Prochenko to the back burner, and I could swear I still smelled her coconut and lime scent.

It was wishful thinking.

For the first time in a long time, I hadn't wanted to get out of bed. I'd almost been late to the briefing, thanks to my need to be near her. That gravitational pull that I couldn't fight anymore.

Leaving her to come deal with a South African drug runner, Logan Brodick, who had kidnapped the daughter of an oil tycoon, Max Teller, had put me in a shite mood. The American government couldn't be involved in this situation for political reasons, so Exodus had been tasked to collect her.

Brodick planned to auction her off to the highest bidder. The girl was only twelve. What the fuck was wrong with people?

On the monitor, Curtis signaled that it was my turn to

speak, so I stood at the head of the table, looking at the other agents around me. They were all good men. I'd worked with most of them on missions before. The only one I didn't really know was Matt Williams. He was from the Canadian Secret Service. Pretty quiet, but he did his job and did it well.

"All right, so we have the location of the girl. This is the compound."

I clicked the remote and accessed the map. "The girl is the priority. We would like to capture Brodick, but that's not priority number one. The girl's safe recovery is, so we don't go in hot. I repeat," I said as I glanced at Rhodes, "we do not go in hot."

Rhodes threw up his hands. "Fuck, you know how to cripple someone's hard-on, don't you?"

I rolled my eyes. "Team one, you'll go in here." I pointed on the monitor to the east entrance. "Supported to the south by team two. Team three, you'll be on the west side. You will have the difficult task of clearing us an exit. We cannot leave the scene in the same way we came in."

One of the other agents, Bill Garret, raised his hand. "Right, who's getting the girl out?"

I nodded. "One of you will need to get her to me over here," I marked the spot on the map, "and we will all exit that way. The rest of you," I circled another egress route, "will go out this way. Hopefully, they won't be chasing you. But if we're discovered and they give chase, that's where they'll go to follow you, and we will get the girl out through the other egress point. There is an airstrip over here, about five clicks out." I pointed to the northern end of the compound.

There were nods all around. Matt Williams raised his hand. "You're not going in?"

"No, I'll stay out this time around."

Curtis nodded on screen. "We all have our roles."

Matt scowled at me, and I frowned. What the fuck was that about? I barely knew the bloke.

"Any other questions?"

There was silence around the table, so I continued. "Updates are on your tablets. We know the auction will happen in forty-eight hours, and they're planning for it to be live and in person. There will be some heavy hitters present as well. Again, their capture is not our immediate concern. We are planning to go in tomorrow, the day before the auction, when we know for sure they will have the girl on the premises. If other targets can be captured that's fine, but if it turns into a firefight, we have clearance to eliminate them. But I'll remind you again that the safe extraction of the girl is our prime directive."

Everyone nodded their assent, and then I ended the meeting.

When Rhodes stood, he grinned at me. "Look at you, leading mission briefs and everything."

I rolled my eyes. "I've been doing this for months."

"Yeah, you have. But you're starting to settle into your skin a little. The look is good on you, mate."

I lifted a brow. "Ah, you slipped into a mate there."

Rhodes frowned. "Fuck. Don't tell Curtis. He'll make me go in for retraining."

No one ever wanted to go back for retraining. Two retraining sessions and you were removed from assignment. Rumor was that when agents were decommissioned that way, no one ever saw them again.

It worked in everyone's favor if you lived and breathed your training and had zero slips.

Rhodes had nothing to worry about with me. I knew he

was solid. "You're fine, mate. Question for you. What's Matt's problem? He seemed displeased when he asked me that question."

"He's miffed about the mission at the Bacchanal. And he went to Curtis about it."

I frowned. "Why?"

"He said you were distracted. Off mission script. If it makes you feel better, I don't think it's personal. He had a partner die six months ago. Jack something or other."

I frowned. "Jack Abbott was his partner?"

Rhodes nodded. "Yeah. The mission lead had other shit going on, and he lost his focus. Jack got killed. So Matt's probably just putting you through your paces."

"Bloody fantastic. All right, I'll deal with him later."

He nodded. "Were you distracted at the Bacchanal though?"

Yes. I'd been worried about Lyra. "No, I wasn't distracted."

"You sure? Your new girlfriend wasn't a distraction?"

I stopped and stared. "For months, you, Michael, Curtis, Command, everyone has been riding me to get with the program. Get settled with someone and evened out. And what, now you're giving me the third degree?"

He shoved his hands in his pockets. "Look, a partner is meant to be your show piece. The pressure release valve. You can't pick someone you actually *want* an emotional connection with. Fuck them all you want, but you need someone you can compartmentalize. You're not meant to fucking fall in love and shit. You clock?"

I frowned at that. I did clock what he was saying. I just had no interest in it. "I like her. There's something about her, but I'm not falling for her."

Liar.

"Good. Then you won't mind a double date."

"With you and Pam? No thank you."

He chuckled low. "It's not a request, bro." He was back to his Americanisms.

My gut clenched. "Fuck. Seriously?"

Rhodes shrugged. "Yeah man, I'm sorry. After the mission, I'm supposed to do an assessment for Curtis. See if this woman is capable of compromising you."

"The target got away, but she had nothing to do with it." I realized my voice was rising, and I quickly modulated.

"Yes, it happens. Don't worry about it. Like you said, she's easy and accessible. Not a big deal. Curtis is just dotting his I's and crossing his T's."

But I didn't like it. They were assessing my relationship with Lyra.

So, it's a relationship?

Fuck. This wasn't a big deal. I liked her. She was fun. I could do this, have a personal life and work too. It was the first time I'd even considered that. Ever. So I'd make it work. And I'd warn her ahead of time. But how? What to say? I needed to check myself. As much as I wanted her, there could be no falling in love here.

You keep telling yourself that you can control that.

I *did* control that, because not falling in love with her was the thing that was going to save her life.

Or you could stop seeing her completely.

Absolutely not. I'd been pushed into this. I hadn't wanted it. But now that I had her, no one was taking her away from me. I'd figure out a solution because I wasn't giving her up. And Command was just going to have to get with the program.

"Lyra, don't make me tell you twice. Retrieval of the girl is your first directive. And I repeat, we're not to terminate the target. We want him alive. Do you understand me?"

I sighed as I triple-checked my weapons. "I hear you. Don't kill him. Yup. Take him to the black site. I understand."

"You're to deliver him to me yourself, Lyra."

I sighed. "Yes, ma'am. Jesus, I heard you. I'm not going to go off book. It's not like I'm in wet work."

James, our wet work specialist on the assignment, muttered under his breath, "You wish."

I could hear the exasperation in Roz's voice over the comms. "God, you're always so obstinate."

"You know, you coached me. So I feel like you had a hand in this."

With a sigh, she added, "Could you try to be, you know, *less* obstinate?"

"And what would be the fun in that?"

When I was ready, I rolled out of the van, gave Addie the peace-out sign, and then closed the door behind me.

We found the compound where the auction was to take place, and while it looked like a beautiful secluded mansion, I knew it had more security than a military stronghold.

My avenue to enter was the maintenance entrance at the side. Security was focused on what was coming out, not what was going in. According to our schematics, this entrance would wind through the gardens and lead me to the servants' quarters. From there, along the east side, was the laundry delivery area. All I had to do was follow the corridors leading into the main house.

The place had been built in the 50s when people still wanted their servants out of the way.

It had been remodeled, according to the blueprints that we had, but not much had been changed.

On the comms, Addie's voice was clear. "Comm check."

I adjusted my earpiece. "I hear you loud and clear, Addie. I am here at the north entrance."

Tyler's voice was low. "Roger. I'm watching your six, Lyra."

"What? That's a first." The words slipped past my lips of their own volition. I knew it was immature, but he was here, on my turf, messing with my controlled world.

Roz's voice cut through sharply. "Take your grievances offline. Right now, we have work to do."

I winced. She was clearly tense about this mission. I was too, but she wasn't acting like herself. I'd talk to her about it later.

At the side entrance, I scowled when I spotted a padlock that hadn't been there two days ago when I'd scouted. "Houston, we have a slight problem. I'm going to improvise though."

"What's wrong?" Roz asked, her voice filled with apprehension.

"There's a padlock on the side door now. A good one."

The litany of curses spewing from Roz's mouth was unusual. "For fuck's sake."

"It's okay. I have this."

On my hip, I had a retractable grappling hook. I stood back ten feet and shot it over the edge of the wall, as close to the hedges as I could manage. If I could use the hedges as cover and climb over, I'd be in.

"Okay, Addie, hit the lights."

Thanks to the excessive heat in LA county, Addie had been giving the area rolling blackouts all day in order to mask my entrance that evening. All of the lights in a five-mile radius went out.

With a running leap toward the wall, I hooked in and started to climb.

It wasn't excessively high. Just ten feet. But it felt like a mountain. Every step I took, I cursed at whoever had put a padlock on that door. When I got to the top, I jumped down, concealed by the mass of overgrown hedges.

I unhooked the grappling hook, retracted it, then hooked it back at my belt before sliding around to a window. A quick check told me no one was inside nearby, so I took out my glass cutter and made a hole large enough for me to climb through without a sound.

Addie's voice was low and steady. "Okay, a minute and thirty seconds until guard swap."

Okay, I could do this. I just had to move quickly and quietly. Each guard had a twelve-hour shift, and each shift included three station rotations. We'd come during mid-shift while they switched stations. They'd be less alert. At least, that was the plan.

With the glass cut, I pulled it down, then set it at the base of the building, my feet sinking a little on the wet grass. The sprinklers must have been run recently. Or maybe they had been going off when we cut the power.

With a deep breath, I hoisted myself up the wall, and through the hole I'd cut in the window. "Okay. I'm in the structure. Which door do I take from here?"

"Second on the left."

I glanced around and saw what I was looking for, and I moved with quiet precision.

"I'm in."

Addie acknowledged. "Excellent. You have a minute left."

Okay, a minute. I could do this. I could absolutely, positively do this. I just had to stay calm.

On my comm unit, Tyler's voice said, "Okay, guards in the north wing have been dealt with. I have their comms."

Good, so Tyler had taken care of them.

Roz's voice was clear. "Team C, report."

Chris, the lead on team C, came back. "All clear. Target one is out."

Once I was in the main part of the house, I tapped my comm unit again. "Okay, I'm in the main house. Where am I going?"

"You need to go up to the third floor. You'll have a guard nearby on your way. He's in the east corridor. Once you take him out, stick him in the little closet to your right, and then you'll be clear for the third floor and the girl. They're keeping her behind the last door on the right."

Easy. Done. I was light on my feet in the dark, waiting for any hint that something was amiss.

The guard was, in fact, in the east corridor. I was quick and quiet, and before he knew what happened, I reached up behind him, injected cyclobenzaprine into his neck, and quickly spun out of the way into the shadows. He winced and cursed, cupping a hand over the injection spot, and then... *Five, four, three, two...*

He went down like a sack of potatoes.

"Jesus, Roz, that's some fast-acting stuff."

"Stop wasting time and go get her."

I had just managed to wrangle the guard into the closet, when Addie's voice said, "Stand down. Stand down. We have hostiles. I repeat, we have hostiles coming in from the east."

My heart leaped and hammered against my ribcage. "Addie? Sit rep?"

"Teams A, C, and E, hold pattern. I repeat, hold pattern."

"What the fuck?" I breathed.

Addie's voice was tight. "I'm trying to figure it out. Hold on."

There was more cursing from Roz.

Tyler's voice came over the line, and he was panting, like he'd been running and was very out of breath. "Fuck. These guys are Exodus."

I heard him grunting and growling. "I took out one hostile. How many more do we have, Addie?"

"Motherfucker, I don't know. They're coming in. Too many of them. Seven? Nine?"

Roz shouted at her. "You need to be sure."

"We have no infrared, so no night vision. I'm doing the best that I can here."

I forced myself to stop, step into the shadows, take a breath, and assess the map on my tablet again. There was nothing but hostiles between me and the girl. "Roz? Advise."

Roz's voice was stern. "Stay put. For the love of God, stay fucking put."

MARCUS

"Comm check."

"Team one, we are go."

"Team two, we are go."

We went through teams three and four, and everything was a go. The mission was simple; go in and rescue the girl. Catching Logan Brodick would be a bonus, but it was secondary to safely retrieving the girl.

Max Teller was powerful and could easily pay the ransom. But why were we doing this and not some kidnap and ransom crew? This was such bullshit.

Get your head in the game.

I had to. I had no other choice.

"Team two, you're in."

Team two entered from the east. "Boss, there are no guards at this entrance."

I frowned at that as I entered through the south, where I also found not a single guard.

What the fuck?

Matt Williams was on team three. "Are we sure we're not walking into a trap?"

"Right now, I don't know what the fuck we're walking into. Proceed with caution. All teams, red alert."

Something didn't feel right. I could feel it in my bones.

"Command, what do we have on the girl?"

Michael was running things remotely from the threat assessment room at headquarters. "I still see a single heat signature in that room. It's her. Minimal movement, but movement all the same. She's alive."

Rhodes came alongside me, and he pulled up his night vision goggles. "Doesn't this strike you as eerie? Like we're not the only operatives here?"

I squinted at him. "The Firm?"

He shrugged. "I wouldn't put it past them."

"All teams, be on high alert. Prepare for Firm operatives." To Rhodes, I said quietly, "How much worse could this get?"

Rhodes laughed. "If I were you, I wouldn't ask that question."

There was static on the line and then something that sounded like a grunt. Michael said, "All teams, report in."

They all did, except for team one.

"Team one, I repeat, report in."

More static.

Rhodes rolled his eyes. "Fuck. I'll go check."

"Team one, Turbo coming to your location. I repeat, Turbo to your location."

At least they wouldn't be alone. I proceeded cautiously up the stairs. I knew the girl was being held on the third floor, but what was that sound?

You're paranoid.

Better to be paranoid than dead.

Rhodes's voice came over the comms. "Yeah. Be very alert. We're not alone, boys and girls."

Fuck, how did The Firm know about our mission?

"Are they after the girl too?"

Michael responded, "It could be."

I tapped into channel A. "Curtis, come in."

"I hear you loud and clear, Phoenix. Sit rep?"

"Confirming, we have Firm operatives onsite."

Curtis's curse was low but heated. "Son of a bitch. How many?"

"No idea. We walked into a silent compound. Lights were off in half the surrounding neighborhoods. We thought it was rolling blackouts, but now this seems like it was set up. Rhodes just checked in. He said the guards are out."

Curtis cursed. "Do you want to abort?"

I glanced up the stairs as I waited for Rhodes to return. Fuck. "No, continue. I'm keeping all teams on alert though."

I switched back to open comms and gave everyone their instructions. "Proceed with extreme caution. Use live rounds carefully. The girl is still on location, be advised."

The footsteps up the stairs had me tucking into my hideout around the corner. But Rhodes's sharp whistle told me it was him. I put my hand out, and sure enough, he whispered, "Did I scare you, princess?"

"Shut up."

I hand-signaled him up the stairs. He would take the corner, I would provide cover, and then I would take the lead.

Once we were up the third flight of stairs, step after careful step led us to the landing, and we moved quickly. Then I heard something.

I gave Rhodes the signal for stop, and he lifted a brow. *What's wrong?* he mouthed.

I frowned back toward the stairs. None of the other teams were supposed to be up here.

I stood at the end of the corridor. Using my hand, I signaled for him to get the girl while I covered the stairs.

He frowned at me, motioning that we should stick together.

I shook my head and tapped my nose, letting him know that I smelled trouble.

He sighed and nodded, taking the command.

Once I saw that he was already halfway down the hall, I headed to the right and eased toward that corner. Something wasn't right. Something felt off. What was behind door number one right here?

Quickly, I rounded to the far side of the door, so that when I opened it, I wouldn't be giving whoever was behind the door a wide-open target.

I dragged in three long breaths to steady my heart rate. I reached for the knob, turned it, then shoved it open. The person inside wasted no time. They came flying out, stun gun first. It was interesting that they weren't using live rounds. Why?

Was this The Firm? And had they come for the girl or for us?

Our rival agencies had been battling for jobs for years. Occasionally, we crossed paths, though it had been happening more and more often of late. Usually, we tended to take different jobs. What was their interest here?

You can think about that when you're not getting your ass kicked.

My attacker was small. Slight. About five foot seven. They were padded with tactical gear, but the fighter was likely a woman. When the Taser hit nothing, the fighter whirled around to my spot, stun gun ready to aim, but I blocked it. I threw a punch to the face, but they dodged it easily with a hand slide along my arm and then dropped to a knee.

Fuck.

My opponent disarmed me with a quick flick of the wrist, then a sneaky elbow to the face had me seeing stars.

This was a woman. No doubt about it. And that scent... I smelled coconuts.

No. No, I did *not* smell coconuts. Lyra had managed to even contaminate my thoughts now... of all times.

The woman wasn't going to let me go, though. She stood between me and the target at the end of the hall. I knew Rhodes could do his job. I didn't like leaving him open though. Because how many of her friends were here?

Yeah, it was definitely a woman. She blocked another hit, but instead of doing the obvious and aiming another knee, she flipped around and delivered a hammer fist to my temple which had me seeing stars. Again.

Fuck. Okay, enough bullshit. If she was aiming to kill, so could I.

The way she moved was familiar, as if I'd fought her before. Maybe all too familiar?

She telegraphed the next kick that came for me, but she still got me right in the ribs. I managed to offset my weight and grabbed her thigh, then I turned my body and tilted my hip out, which sent her careening down.

When I dove for her, she rolled away easily, attacking back with a hammer kick. One that I had to rapidly roll away from. Christ.

She dove for me then with her fists and elbows. We ended up rolling around, and I thought again about how familiar this felt. I caught her arms in my grip and said, "Stop fucking moving."

Under her mask, her brows furrowed and then lifted. She blinked twice, and then dropped her head away from me.

"Be still. I'm not going to—" I didn't get to finish my sentence because she brought her head back then snapped it forward with a head butt. "Bugger."

She did it again, and then she managed to wiggle out of my arms and tried to deliver another cracking elbow, which I blocked. But blocking her, unfortunately, forced me to let her go. She sprung back to her feet in a lithe movement. Like a jack rabbit.

Why was she so familiar?

"Do I know you?" I asked.

She cocked her head as we danced around. From the end of the hall, I heard gunshots, and my heart seized. "Fucking Rhodes."

While my attention was split, my assailant reached behind my neck and hit me with a fucking taser, and the electrical charge shot up my arm. "Motherfucker."

As electrical shocks crawled through my skin, I ground my teeth as it took me to my knees.

But what was interesting was that even as the edges of my vision started to gray, she didn't shoot me. Instead, she turned and headed down the hallway toward Rhodes and those gunshots we'd both heard.

I refused to go down. I couldn't.

Instead, I pushed to my feet. I had to stop her.

I watched as she ran, and I knew I'd seen that gait before. Oh God. There was no way. There was *no fucking way*.

I reached for her and then dove at her feet, taking her down.

She struggled to get free, body flailing, trying to break out of my hold. Jesus Christ, she was a good fighter.

Lyra. She smelled like Lyra.

My conscious brain fought it. There was no way. This was not who I thought it was.

When I was on top of her, I grasped an arm, even as she tried to punch me with the other one and I dodged it. "Hold still, I'm not going to hurt—"

And before I knew it, she planted her feet, lifted her hips, and rolled us both over with her on top. With her free arm, she punched me straight in the trachea.

As I wheezed and coughed, she aimed at it again, but this time I blocked it, even as I was fighting for air.

I was forced to let her go as I scrambled to breathe, and she was up on her feet like lightning, trying to get around me. I snapped one arm around her ankle and tugged her back down.

She let out a wail. "Ahh."

It couldn't be her. Please, God, no. But I had to find out for sure.

I tugged her back even as she whipped around with another kick. She missed her mark though. She'd been aiming for the groin, I could tell, but instead, she got my gut. It wasn't a picnic, but it wasn't debilitating either.

I dragged her under my body. "Hold bloody still, or I will hurt you."

She still struggled.

"I'm going to take this mask off of you." She shook her head back and forth, fighting, clawing, and I knew. I knew what I was going to find, but I still had to know for sure. I reached for her mask, pulled it up, and lifted it partway off her face. It revealed lips that I was very well acquainted with.

LYRA

Oh *God. Oh God. Oh God.*

He'd started to pull off my mask as I fought his hold. The mask only made it up to my nose before I reached my arm up straight over my head and smashed it down on his hand, right at the wrist, forcing him to loosen his grip. I raised my hips, rolled him over, and landed a punch that was hard enough to stun him as I reached for the weapon he'd dropped.

With my finger on the trigger, I pressed my comm unit hard. "I have an assailant. Third floor hallway. Status check."

Addie's voice was sharp. "What happened to your goddamn comms? We have the girl. I repeat, we have the girl. All teams, exit now."

My team had her.

And Marcus is Exodus.

I had my gun pointed at his chest, and deep down I knew I just hadn't *wanted* to see it. And Christ, I didn't know what to do or what to say. We just froze in position there in the hallway, staring at each other.

On channel B, I called out, "Addie?"

"Yeah, are you getting out of there? Your exit is south exit. Proceed there ASAP. We still have Exodus agents in there."

"Addie," my voice wheezed out.

"What? What is it, Lyra? Are you injured?"

"No. I have an Exodus agent in front of me."

"Is he dead?"

"No. He's alive."

I'd thought it was just us on B channel, but Roz's voice came in loud and clear.

"What's the problem, Lyra?"

I forced myself to repeat the words that slashed at my heart. "I—I have an Exodus agent."

He peered at me from where he knelt, hands by his side. I'd dragged my mask back down, but he knew. He absolutely knew. So what was the point? Finally, I reached up and pulled it over my head so I could fucking breathe.

My heart pumped so hard, flooding my blood with adrenaline. I didn't know what to do.

On the ground, Marcus scowled at me as he reached for his own mask.

I shook my head at him. "No, you don't. No suicide pills."

"Easy does it, love. I'm just taking off my mask."

I cocked my gun, but he was telling the truth. All he did was remove his mask. His handsome jawline came into view first. And even in this situation, my pussy clenched.

Oh fuck. Fuck. Fuck. Fuck.

All the pieces fell together, finally making sense. All of them. As I watched the man whom I'd started to care about take his mask off, I could see so clearly all those moments. The way he'd stood between me and Prochenko, his insistent demand on self-defense training, and him teaching me skills I already had. Skills all Firm *and* Exodus agents had.

Two sides of the same coin.

"Lyra, you know what to do here. We'll both walk away and we both stay alive."

"Are you kidding me? You're a dead man."

"I'm not if you don't tell anyone."

It suddenly occurred to me what was going to happen to my life. I couldn't go home because he would tell everyone who I was. Once again, I was that girl with no home, no family, nowhere to go. No safety.

I wanted to cry. "Why did it have to be you?"

"*Me?* Why did it have to be *you?* At any point, you could have told me, and I would have *helped* you."

"Helped me what? Stop doing my job? I'm not an assassin. Is that what you think? That I'm an assassin? I'm a government agent, just like you."

He gave me a dismissive laugh. "Oh, right. Firm agents are assassins for hire. Everyone knows that."

"Is that what they told you? We're two sides of the same coin, Marcus. I'm not an assassin. We're field operators, that's all."

"So you say. How many hits have you performed?"

"What? Is that something to brag about?"

"How many, Agent Wilkinson?"

I frowned at that. "How many have *you* done? You are Exodus, after all. Let me guess, from the looks of you, you're ex-military, plucked out at your peak for the most top-secret missions."

"You don't know what you're talking about."

I rolled my eyes. "Don't I? We work for two sides of what was once the same organization, but they're in competition now. Whatever you've been told about me, don't believe it. Just like I don't believe you're an assassin. But I do believe you're a good little soldier, and that given the opportunity, you would kill me."

He winced. "You think I could do that? Kill you? After everything?"

"I think you're capable of it." My gun didn't waver. I switched back to B channel and said, "Control, advise."

Roz's voice was stern. "We don't need him. Eliminate him."

The bottom fell out of my stomach. "Repeat? Bad copy. Repeat."

My mentor, my friend, the only mother figure I'd had in the last six years through my training and then my time as a field agent had just told me to kill the man that I—

What? You love?

"I—"

"Agent Wilkinson? Lyra, am I clear?"

"Clear."

I switched channels and turned off the comms. "Marcus, I'm sorry."

He frowned at me as he pushed to his feet, and I backed up one step. "You can't shoot me anymore than I could shoot you. We can both walk away. Put the gun down, Lyra."

"What, I put the gun down and you take that knife at the small of your back and slice my jugular?"

"No. I won't do that. I never even reported to my Command that you'd seen Prochenko's face."

My voice was small. "You didn't?"

He shook his head. "Let me guess, you didn't report that I had either?"

I shook my head. "I have my orders."

"Fuck your orders. Think for yourself. You know me. I've

held you in my arms." He slapped his palm on his chest. "You. Know. Me."

Tears fell from my eyes. "Fuck. Marcus, stop."

"Lyra, I—"

I fired.

I had been aiming for his shoulder, right below the clavicle where the musculature was fleshy.

But what if that's not what you hit?

I didn't have time to check. The look on his face as I fired and turned to go... the shock, the horror, the betrayal... It was not a look I would soon forget.

FIND out how Lyra handles the ultimate betrayal in The Assassin in 5F...

ABOUT NANA MALONE

USA Today Best Seller, Nana Malone's love of all things romance and adventure started with a tattered romantic suspense she "borrowed" from her cousin.

It was a sultry summer afternoon in Ghana, and Nana was a precocious thirteen. She's been in love with kick butt heroines ever since. With her overactive imagination, and channeling her inner Buffy, it was only a matter a time before she started creating her own characters.

Now she writes about sexy royals and smokin' hot bodyguards when she's not hiding her tiara from Kidlet, chasing a puppy who refuses to shake without a treat, or begging her husband to listen to her latest hairbrained idea.

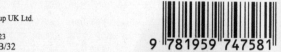

Ingram Content Group UK Ltd.
Milton Keynes UK
UKHW042144050523
421281UK00004B/32